Tommy is a thirteen-year-old M.
Manchester United and the video   ...iuse idea
of a foreign holiday is taunting fans ɴom rival clubs across
the Channel.

One day he is plucked from school by his mother,
Poppy, to join her in a bronchial old Bedford bound for
Kathmandu. En route he is exposed to a bewildering
array of characters and cultures, and to a series of
unforgettable experiences. He is regaled by gipsies in
Austria, sleeps in a Roman necropolis in Turkey, visits the
weird region of Cappodocia with its ancient underground
cities, narrowly escapes stone-throwing rioters in Pakistan, meets a sinister magician in Delhi – a 'city aswirl
with sorcery' – and witnesses a wedding on a Kashmiri
houseboat, during which the bridegroom expires. By the
time they get to Kathmandu, Tommy is no longer the kid
for whom goal posts are the only landmarks worthy of
notice . . .

Suitable for fourteen-year-olds upwards, *Tommy
Granite* is both an earthily funny, fast-moving, utterly
absorbing travel story and the story of the inner
transformation of a child.

Born in North Lincolnshire in 1949, Jay Ravendale was
inspired at an early age by tales of his uncle's life in India
and subsequently spent the next 20 years funding trips
overseas with the proceeds of his English and drama
teaching. He was runner-up in the Montagne Jeunesse
travel writing competition with an entry based on life in
the Turks and Caicos Islands. Recent successes included
Hitched, a musical for youth theatre, and *Down the
Tube,* a hard-hitting one-act play about solvent abuse
that was featured on the BBC. He has also published a
series of travel articles in the *Grimsby Evening Telegraph.*

Jay Ravendale is married with one child, also called
Jay. He is currently working on a full-length adult play
and is researching for new material in Vietnam and
Cambodia.

TOMMY GRANITE

Jay Ravendale

The Book Guild Ltd
Sussex, England

The Book Guild Ltd
25 High Street
Lewes, Sussex

First published 1995
© Jay Ravendale 1995
Set in Souvenir Light
Typesetting by Dataset Typesetting & Origination
St. Leonards-on-Sea

Printed in Great Britain by
Athenaeum Press Ltd
Gateshead

A catalogue record for this book is
available from the British Library

ISBN 0 86332 979 9

CONTENTS

1

ENGLAND

The alarm cancanned a full five inches along Tommy Granite's bookshelf before catapulting onto his duvet. It flew over the giant Schmeichel's outstretched hands, nutmegged Pallister and embedded itself somewhere in the region of Bryan Robson's groin. A hideous, muffled whine followed.

Further along the landing, Poppy, Tommy's mum, moaned deliciously as she moulded her body into the rippling, hairy shape of Tommy's dad. Strands of her own hair, greying now, braided with her husband's to form a soft, downy mattress. She slid an arm over a fleshy, matted shoulder and planted a drowsy kiss upon an unsuspecting earlobe.

The pair of them, Poppy and Tommy, were away quickly, sucked into a black cab and swept off to the station. John Oliver Granite slumbered on, as arranged, sprawled over his wife's warm, recently vacated space, hugging the indentations as if she were still there. 'Jog' had a job, running the local leisure centre, and there was no way he could slide off for a year.

The clerk's face relaxed slightly as she came to the Granites' application. Soccer starlet or not, at thirteen Tommy was still classed as a dependant, too young to wave his own documents at hatchet-faced border guards cracking down on undeclared talent. Poppy's flowery

7

strokes embraced them both, making the clerk forget momentarily those butcher boys and slaughterhouse workers hell-bent on sweaty stays in Torremolinos. In the best traditions of Raleigh, Hillary and Indiana Jones, Poppy dispelled the prospect that outside the passport office nothing existed save a vast abattoir.

NAMES: POPPY AND TOMMY GRANITE
OCCUPATIONS: ADVENTURERS
PROPOSED DESTINATIONS: EVERYWHERE

The first three months of Tommy's trip would transport him to the Himalayan kingdom of Nepal, the snowy home of Everest. Poppy had paid £1000 each for truck space on a bronchial old Bedford, along with a couple of dozen others who had opted to shelve the predictability of their lives for the time being.

For some, that had meant wobbling unsteadily out of building society doors or supermarkets or nurses' homes after all the send-offs and farewell parties.

For Poppy too, it celebrated the end of a long flirtation with the working week, years of throwing clay about in dusty old rooms with high windows. She'd had time out to raise Jim, reduced now to a buried statistic in a coroner's file, just as she had had later for Tommy. Her potter's wheel had slowed to its final halt at an educational greenhouse on a browning campus when early retirement came along.

For Tommy, wrenching himself away from routine had had more serious consequences. It meant missing an entire season for a start, at a time when the Reds were going through a period of self-doubt and needed all the support they could muster. Jog had promised to mail on all reports, though, via poste restante, and he had bought him a short-wave radio to pick up the lugubrious

8

tones of James Alexander Gordon every Saturday at 5 p.m., adjustable according to whichever time zone Tommy happened to be in.

There were other drawbacks to bunking off for a year, of course. He'd have no idea who was in the charts, he'd miss his mates from the Youthie, particularly Flegg and Grobbo, and he'd never catch up with Baldwin's shenanigans in 'The Street'.

But there were compensations. No more being holed up with Miss Brown twice a week to hammer out scales in her antimacassared lounge. No more oral gymnastics from Mr Mengele, the family dentist, whose bloody prowess with the drill would have been the envy of a construction site. And, of course, for one entire, glorious year . . . no more school.

'You'll probably be the only kid on the trip, Tom,' Poppy informed him, as they were swallowed up into the Underground. 'Don't build your hopes up.'

'As long as they don't try giving me children's portions at chow time. Big plate for you, little plate for me,' he added sardonically.

'I'm forty two,' observed the bushy individual sitting to Poppy's right, en route to Victoria, 'and that's all I've ever known. Children's portions throughout life. Happiness, love . . .'

'Come on, Tommy. I think there's a shade more space further down the carriage. Pick up your things.' She urged him brightly towards the emergency doors.

'Don't expect more,' the philosopher hollered after them gloomily.

Poppy had chosen a company called Last Exit to deliver them safely up in Kathmandu. Its expedition members were to gather at Suffolk Plaza, a faded, fenced-off rectangle of scrub where cider and sherry bottles jockeyed for position.

'Well, this is the place.' Poppy hunched up her shoulders in excitement. 'What an atmosphere! Full of character! Looks like we're first.' She dropped to her haunches, extracted a tissue to push about her spectacles then began expertly to peel an orange. Tommy leaned back against the fencing, coolly hooking his thumbs into the seat of his 501s.

A solitary figure, though, drew their attention as he scythed across the traffic, his mackintosh billowing wildly in his wake. He might have been forty and his eyes shone. His mouth hung open and Tommy couldn't help noticing the trademarks of Mr Mengele, or a similarly gifted practitioner, glinting from within. One claw clutched a supermarket trolley, the other a can of Special Brew.

'Well, hello,' Poppy piped, rising from the ground to proffer a dripping, fruity segment in his direction. 'Have some. It's wonderful. Are you on the trip too?'

'Lady,' he snarled, before careering off into the bushes, 'I've been on the trip since 1968.'

Tommy was a sharp-looking kid, alert and tallish for his age, though a shade skinny. All knobbly knees and pencil elbows, his mum said. He didn't get his ginger hair from either Poppy or his dad, which led periodically to tiresome jokes about the milkman. His eyes were strong and blue and they held your gaze, especially if you were an opponent in the Mancunian Colts' league. They hadn't been used on girls to the same effect yet, those eyes, but Louise reasoned that that was only a matter of time. Louise was a year below Tommy at school and, although they'd never spoken, her knowledge of him was comprehensive. She'd slipped a Good Luck card into his locker on the final day, with two kisses planted inside, one for each of his pale, clear cheeks. Anonymously, of course. Time was on her side. Louise could wait a year.

By mid-afternoon, a dusty pyramid of rucksacks lay

stacked across the kerb. A good proportion of them sported badges of the Aussie flag, being brandished by a particularly violent-looking kangaroo. Their owners sprawled about the pavement, making easy conversation. The loudest, an irregular-shaped girl with a grainy complexion and a preposterous bosom, hailed Tommy as she might an old drinking companion.

'You following the cricket, kid?'

Painfully, he wrenched his eyes away from her hopelessly inadequate vest and engaged his thought processes.

'Pardon?'

'Cricket. What's the latest?'

Gulping like a goldfish, Tommy raised his eyes to meet those of his first live Australian.

'Dunno, sorry. I play football.'

She smiled unnervingly, tilting a can of Coke over the rucksacks.

'No worries. Just thought you might know. Fancy a drink?'

Poppy's greatest fear had been of playing Granny-goes-on-Holiday. Adventure holidays for the 18-30s, the brochure had said, and neither she nor Tommy fitted into that category, even remotely. Maybe people figured you were too young for adult fun before eighteen and too old for it after thirty. However, she'd waved a cheque and the company had waived the rules.

She needn't have worried. There were a few weedy-looking married couples, white and doleful, draped about their suitcases and a couple of young pups straight out of university. They'd have been about Jim's age had he, you know, been given the chance. A demure Swiss girl kept her own company by the fencing, nursing a backpack decorated with the red-and-white of her national flag. On the far side of rucksack mountain, a

11

family busied itself distributing malaria tablets. The father, a restless figure in Aussie whites, looked for all the world as if he'd left his own course of treatment too late. He was broad and athletic but his skin was already awash with perspiration. His wife, a dumpy, jolly woman, popped a pill onto her tongue and called cheerily over to Tommy.

'G'day. Are you listening to the Test?'

Their daughter took the last of the tablets. She looked to be at that certain age when parents can still say what goes though all parties concerned know it's not going to be for much longer. Sixteen, maybe seventeen. She sported a rugby shirt, open at the collar, and the brown waves of her hair fell over it. Pleasant-looking, Poppy thought uncharitably, but just misses being pretty. She watched as the girl's eyes swam over the group, rested momentarily on Tommy, and then moved on again.

Without warning, a works coach cut in beside them with the sort of gear change you associate with parrots being throttled. Its driver, a shockhaired, roly-poly Scot, looked to have leapt directly from a kids' comic. As if someone had taken a pre-war bicycle pump to the backside of Dennis the Menace and built up a decent sweat.

'I'm with Last Exit,' he leered, 'and this, ladies and gentlemen, is your executive coach to Dover. Hop on.'

Tommy's last trip across the Channel had been with the school, the previous Easter. It held vivid memories of taunting a rival group of pubescents from Cologne, embarking on an English exchange. 'Four-two, four-two,' his mates had chanted, waving arms and pointing rigid little fingers at their perplexed opposition. All this, despite the fact that not one of them had been born on that balmy summer's evening in 1966. It was a long way to have to go back to record a victory. The teachers had nipped further developments in the bud once they'd

12

eluded the queues at Duty Free.

After hoisting a couple of humongous-sized Toblerones upon his shoulder, Tommy drifted over the ship's arcades, passing a pleasant hour and a half in the company of Pacman and Street Ninja. He emerged three quid lighter as the ferry pulled into Zeebrugge.

2

CONTINENTAL DRIFT

To the mild surprise of the party, the expedition vehicle stood awaiting them at the quayside. It was a twelve-year-old Bedford, one of Last Exit's more recent acquisitions. Two of its tyres were quite sound, the others only bald in patches, and the body work showed no significant signs of rot.

'Wonderful,' breathed Poppy, as she helped roll back the canvas rigging. 'Open sides. All that lovely fresh air!'

Tommy stood below her, gazing up into her flaring nostrils with familiar disgust.

'Mum,' he intoned, tapping the side of his own clean conk by way of elaboration. Surreptitiously, Poppy removed a creeper of Amazonian proportions that dangled nonchalantly to her upper lip.

'Thanks, Tom.' She winked in gratitude. Some people suffered warts or dandruff. Others were distressed by alopecia or piles. Poppy had always been plagued by boogers.

Once the canvas had been securely lashed, the adventurers swarmed over the truck like pirates, shoving their gear into impossible allocations of space. The company's regulations about luggage had been flagrantly disregarded. Day packs, stuffed with Supertampax and defoliants, lay strewn everywhere. Fishing tackle and a ghettoblaster hung loosely from the roof. Tommy stowed his gear next to that of an excitable blond doctor from Alice. He extracted his Walkman, placed the phones over his head, made minor adjustments, and submitted himself to the dubious charms of Happy Mondays.

Further down the truck, the smell of pilchards assailed Poppy's already beleaguered nostrils. She sat wedged between crates of tinned fish and a lardy librarian from Leicester. But before introductions could get formally underway, the engine sprang into life and the truck's assault down the autobahns began. Two more adventurers had yet to be jammed in, a Swiss couple called Bolsterley. They did not, Poppy lamented, as she took her turn to breathe, sound particularly trim.

They pulled in, as dark fell, to one of the picnic areas that dot the motorways every few kilometres. Their courier sprang out of the cab to address his crew.

'We're camping here tonight. It's illegal but it doesn't come much cheaper. It'll save us time and money and we'll need both of those in Asia. Okay, let's get those tents down.'

After three helpings, Tommy decided he never wanted to see pilchards and rice again. He flipped open a can of Coke as the group settled around a couple of picnic benches to raise questions. Poppy, along with a New Zealander in her late twenties, had volunteered to wash the pots and they crouched a few metres away, scrubbing pans by lamplight.

'Haggis,' the driver indicated, poking his ample chest with a podgy forefinger. A bolt of tomato sauce cut across his hooped jumper, a birthday-cum-Christmas present from his mean aunt in Dunfermline. 'I'm with you all the way to Kathmandu.'

'And so am I.' A well-built figure in her early twenties stepped out of the shadows. She'd been with the truck at Zeebrugge and had kept in the cab ever since.

'Sally. Our mechanic and co-driver.'

Even in the faint light, it was possible to see her pink slightly as she stepped back.

'We'll be heading up to Salzburg tomorrow. After that, we'll establish a rota for buying food, cooking and packing the tents. Until then, perhaps you can all chip in and lend a hand.' Haggis paused to search their faces. 'Any questions?'

The plump, owlish librarian pushed herself forward slightly.

'Is it worth changing any money tomorrow?'

Haggis scratched his backside and pondered.

'Not really. We'll be through three countries in three days. Each time you change money you pay commission. Each time you pay commission you get ripped off. I'll lend you enough for a beer. Pay me back later.'

'I'm vigitarian.' Poppy's helpmate had wandered over from the lamplight. A corona of bugs danced about her head. 'Are there iny spicial arrangements for me?'

'Do you like cheese?' Haggis grinned.

Tommy, as if at school, suddenly became aware of his left hand travelling up the side of his body and above his head.

'Er . . .' Heads swivelled round as the night air caught the back of his throat. 'Er . . . how long do we have to go between washes?'

With Sally and Haggis alternating at the wheel, they made 800 'kays' the next day. It was strange how easily the group had slipped into abbreviation. They borrowed 'Dee Ems' from each other, swapped stories about leaving 'Yoo Kay'.

John, the doctor from Alice, became Tommy's tent-mate. It was two to a tent, no singles, and the way it panned out was that Tommy, John, Poppy and the New Zealand girl had been left staring at the remains of the

16

equipment. Tommy hadn't particularly wanted to share with his mum anyway. He felt uneasy pinning her underwear on the washing line back home and the prospect of catching her alive and inside it under canvas filled him with dread. His own body too had, for the last couple of years, been behaving in ways he'd rather she didn't know about. Similarly, John was a perfect stranger to Penny, the Kiwi, and neither wished to take the chance of some unsolicited and unwelcome groping under the dark confines of the canvas. So, by mutual agreement, Tommy had trooped off with John, leaving Poppy and Penny to mutilate their tent pegs beyond recognition.

The arrangement with loo stops was as follows: the rear of the truck was fitted with a buzzer connected to Haggis's cab. One press signalled 'Stop When Convenient'; two presses meant 'Bale Out Now'. As the truck ground towards Salzburg, Tommy totalled the stoppages so far: sixteen, all by females, six of which had been occasioned by Penny. Was there some deep significance to this? Were males too coy to dip into the woods for a quick pee on a tree? It didn't stop them on the motorways, come Saturday, lined up on the hard shoulder behind the coach, teasing the beery drops off their knobs in defiance of passing motorists. Maybe men were bolder in groups. Maybe they'd just got more self-control.

As the truck ground to a halt for the seventeenth time, Penny vaulted desperately over the side. Ominously, she'd hit the buzzer three times. No-one knew for sure what this signified, though a few of the more adventurous were twitching their noses. Beyond her, at the service station, a formidable cleaning woman was blocking the ladies' loo with an array of fast food furniture, upturned at lethal angles. At a more leisurely pace, Tommy sauntered over to the gents, stopping to pick up a discarded DM by

17

the litter bin. At the entrance, he drew back to avoid an ostentatiously-dressed traveller with a green plastic parrot clamped to his shoulder.

Hardly had Tommy hitched his shorts over the porcelain when a harpie's shriek rent the air.

'Lit me in, you fascist bitch!'

'Wegen des waschens ist diese Toilette zegeschlossen.'

In the gents, save for Tommy, blond men continued to peer at the cold urinal.

'I don't care. I'm nearly peeing myself.'

'Es ist verboten während der Reinigungszeit die Toilette zu betreten.'

Tommy rushed eagerly to the entrance, barely pausing to adjust his coiffure, as pandemonium erupted. The man with the plastic parrot stood rapt, some ten metres away. The dough-faced cleaning woman, her hamlike arms twitching, was triumphantly blocking the ladies' passageway, wielding her mop like an obscene cheerleader. Crashing and stumbling against the woman's spiked defences, Penny lunged at the sanitary baton.

'Lit me in, you blockhid!'

'Dieses Gebiet ist zugeschlossen. Bitte kommen Sie in einer halben Stunde zurück, wenn Sie in die Hose nicht geschissen haben.'

Intent on peaceful negotiation, Parrotman suddenly fluttered forward, perching himself between the combatants.

'Excuse me, miss. This area is closed for cleaning. She says you can come back in half-an-hour if you haven't . . . ah . . . inconvenienced yourself by then.' Curiously, as if it were listening, the plastic parrot cocked its head to one side.

Penny's response caused picnickers to pause from their monstrous snacks in the leafy bays on the far side of the autobahn.

'Aaaaaaaaaaaagh! Bollocks!' Her left foot swung back to reveal a pointed boot. Momentarily, Penny held it poised before smashing it with pinpoint precision into her adversary's kneecap. As her legs buckled and bulk sagged, it became the cleaning woman's turn to shriek.

'Aaaaaaaaaaaagh! Scheisskopf!'

Blinded by tears, she whooshed her mop handle round in a lethal, retaliatory arc, though Penny had long gone. With venomous force, it decapitated the winking parrot at a stroke, slashing into the hapless translator's face just above the temple.

With her opponent temporarily disabled, Penny then confounded her audience by tearing into the gents. She burst in, wild-eyed, confronted by six pairs of loosened trousers and lowered zips. Behind her, the raging cleaner threshed about her barricades as Parrotman stooped to blow the dust off the damaged plumage of his plastic pet. Ahead of her, all along the stalls, limp willies were being hiccupped into holsters by their modest owners.

Somewhat fazed, Tommy headed for the cafeteria. Adventurers were disembarking from the truck in ones and twos as what had started as a loo-stop blurred into brunch. Poppy launched herself over the side to comfort a tearful Penny whilst Tommy took himself past the food bar into the video arcade. A knot of intent-looking German boys had commandeered his favourite machine and, hell, could they play! There were no girls and there was no conversation. It was shadowy and the air crackled with electronic noise. They could have been anywhere in Yoo Kay.

Three peeps on the horn sounded and Tommy still had his DM intact. Reluctantly, he tore himself away.

They crossed southern Germany on a Sunday. Despite the harvest, farmers remained at home. There were few trucks on the road. On the far side of the sound barriers, stretches of young pines wilted, stripped and blackened by the ravages of automobile pollution and acid rain. There was not much to look at. Tommy was reminded of the tall industrial stacks of the Lancashire valleys. Each year, the factory owners paid compensation to the farmers whose fields they polluted in Scandinavia.

The prickly subject of nicknames cropped up, from which no-one was to be spared. Haggis was a veritable fund of them, mostly culled from previous trips. He'd baptised a number of 'Ferrets', several 'Spuds' and three 'Toads'. Two obscenely fat sisters had once travelled to Kathmandu, burdened under the soubriquets Jumbo and Michelin Woman. Desperately humiliated, they undertook to shed one hundred kilograms by the time they broached the Nepalese border. They made it. Amidst delirious scenes of drunken revelry, Haggis had them rechristened Pins and Needles.

There had been some agonising over Penny. 'Loostop' had been suggested but Haggis overruled. There was something about the way Kiwis pronounced the letter 'e'. It tended to come out as 'i' as in 'bit'. Thus, Penny, who had taken to advising some of the precocious girls on the dangers of 'premarital six', became forever Pinny.

One of those very girls, the awesome figure in the inadequate vest, saved a substantial amount of time by voicing what had been on everyone's mind. She swung her massive frontage about, causing a slight breeze to ripple through the encampment, and spoke plainly. She had been raised on a remote outpost in Northern Territories where any cissy who paid a woman the compliment of a bouquet of flowers was doomed forever.

'Don't dwell too long on a name for me,' she urged. 'Call me Nokkers. Every other bar-stard does.' She fixed a smile on them for an instant and then pulled on the ring-cap of a beer.

Poppy was another straightforward case.

'Where ya from, Pop?'

Laughter came easily to them, these Australians. They had blended the adventurers together as a group and Tommy liked them.

'Manchester.'

'Niver heard of it.'

Poppy laughed with them.

'Never heard of it! Don't you have *Coronation Street* in Australia?'

'Oh, we have it, Pop. We just don't watch it.'

Marc-Marc leaned over. The adventurers had latched on pretty quickly to his habit of repeating things twice over.

'Here, Tommy, chuck us yer passport. Chuck us yer passport, hey.'

'Bloody hellfire! Granite. Is that yer name?'

It took a second to register. Nokkers got there first, spitting out the contents of a three-day-old buttie.

'Pommy! Pommy Granite! Stone the crows!'

Shortly after pulling into Salzburg, the Bolsterleys arrived. They were even grosser than Tommy feared. Supper had to be re-distributed to accommodate them and everyone lost a spoonful of bolognese.

Food, Tommy could see, might well be a problem during the coming months. He himself had an appetite bordering on the gluttonous which was all right so long as the majority only picked at their food. The problem, to Tommy's irritation, was that the majority did not seem to want to pick at their food. On the contrary, they were exhibiting at that precise moment all the restraint of slum kids on a trolley dash round Sainsbury's. Tommy's gloom deepened. One bragged of going back for sevenses after a fry-up in Africa. His bloated companions had staggered off to decorate the surrounding bush after

21

six helpings apiece, spineless buggers. Tommy shuddered.

As he unpicked congealed spaghetti from the cook pot and sucked it philosophically through pursed lips, Tommy couldn't help noticing the oddballs on the next pitch. They'd have got in for free at a fancy dress, for sure. Their trailer was hitched up to a gleaming Mercedes. Outside, kilos of prime steak lay heaped about their barbecues; enough to keep the adventurers, even the Bolsterleys, going for days.

But what puzzled Tommy was their language. He'd flirted with French and German at school and it didn't sound like those. He'd cultivated an Italian penfriend during the last World Cup and that didn't provide any clues.

'Hey, mister!' The man was middle-aged and he stood over his barbecue, calling Tommy 'mister'. In one hand, he held a groaning platter of aromatic steaks. 'Hey, mister. You and your friends, you want?' Tommy strayed over. People in England didn't give stuff away to strangers. Hell, they'd cross to the other side of the road. With his free hand, the oddball gestured airily in the direction of the truck. 'Take, please. You are young and do not look rich.'

From nowhere, Poppy drifted into the conversation.

'Well, hello. Lovely to see you. Isn't it wonderful here!' She paused to remove a minor blockage discreetly from her left nostril. 'Fabulous views.'

'Mum,' Tommy interposed, pressing a tired-looking tissue into her palm, 'this gentleman wants to give us all this.' He paused to take the weight of two kilos of spiced meat and managed to convey the tone of someone for whom a polite refusal would certainly offend.

Rolf's family were the first Romanies Tommy had met. Gipsies always got bad press in Britain. Like Rolf, they'd forsaken their nags and caravans for motorised trailers but, unlike Rolf, they always seemed on the fringe of trouble. Dirty and thieving was how most people perceived them. All called Smith to fox the DHSS, all shiftless and untrustworthy. Warring with councils, battling with yobs and householders wherever they tried to settle.

'My people had their problems too,' Rolf had told him, breathing out a cloud of wonderfully sweet tobacco. 'In the thirties, I lost nearly everybody. The government killed my parents, my grandparents, my sisters. I spent my life as a young man in the Balkans, hiding in the mountains. Since then, it has been much better.'

He woke on the first buzz of John's alarm and slapped it into silence. Never a great one for washes, Tommy considered that it had now been three days since he'd had his head inside a basin and, to tell the truth, he felt kind of grungey. He'd sprayed the outside of his T-shirt with Brut a couple of times but he still felt sticky. 'Let your armpits be your charmpits,' he intoned to a comatose John and bundled his way down to the showers.

To his dismay, the men's room was temporarily closed. The females, however, showed every sign of being both open and unoccupied. Tommy gazed round, then slid inside.

Apart from the dispensing machine on the wall and a more generous allocation of mirrors, there was little to distinguish the blocks. Tommy stripped quickly and stepped into the end cubicle. The shower activated at the touch of a button and in seconds Tommy was lost in a warm, soapy reverie that featured a post-match splashabout with the United midfield.

'Good of yer to step in at a moment's notice like that, kid.'

'Yeah, nice goal, an' all.'

23

'See the manager took yer name then.'

United had been playing Salzburg in their pre-season Continental tour. Half the team had gone down with food poisoning and on top of that somebody had nicked their kit. It was panic stations. Tommy had dragged Poppy along to the game, even though she wanted to spend time by the river, and when the tannoy came over, he knew it was his big chance.

'. . . so if there are any United supporters out there today, preferably with a first-team strip, could they make themselves known to the match officials.'

Tommy always wore his full kit to first-team games, like a hundred other kids. Under his jeans, of course. You never knew when you'd be called on. Inside ten minutes, he was on the pitch.

A stunning cross-field pass, drawing a smattering of applause from even the home crowd, had just set up United's winger when Nokkers breezed in.

'Hello, Tommy. Communal showers today, is it?'

She took up residence in the cubicle opposite, casting towel, top and knickers aside to join in the soapy exercise. Tommy shrank. Every part of his body shrivelled up as he turned towards the shower head, pushing his face into the jet and into oblivion.

'Hi, Tom.'

'Nokkers.'

The occupants of tent three, Captain Hurricane and his wife, threw their gear onto a bench and stripped off. Cap had been the Australian dispensing malaria tablets back at Suffolk Plaza and this morning he was dispensing soap. Sliding a wicked Bowie knife from its sheath. Cap chopped a bar of unsuspecting Palmolive into equal portions in two swift strokes.

'Here we go, Jenny. Save this piece for Alison.'

And no-one blinked when a couple of Scandinavian

bikers brought their BMW in for a hose-down. They stood it at the end of the cubicle area, regaled in all their leathers, and gazed upon it lovingly. Cap broke off from singing a Victorian bush song to lend them some soap.

After an age Tommy turned round, his eyes drilled to the rivulets chasing across the ceramic floor. Heavily, he lifted his eyes to the area of movement in the cubicle opposite. Nokkers was bludgeoning herself with a sponge, slapping and squeezing, grunting as the soap trickled into her eyes like a stream entering the sea. Her bosom swung as she shifted, re-directing the deltas flowing across it. Droplets hung poised above her nipples for an instant, before falling into the maelstrom below. As he caught his gaze tracking downwards, towards a different type of delta altogether, Tommy pulled himself around guiltily. Better another confrontation with the shower head. Jets pierced his eyes in punishment as, further below, his body conspired to produce an intoxicating mix of pleasure and humiliation. A hardening, a thickening, was setting in at a place where it had no right to, not at this particular time.

'Need an extra towel, love?' Poppy's hand reached into his cubicle and flicked a fleecy, beige remnant from home onto his bench. Without drying himself, without turning, Tommy reached backwards and strapped the towel tightly about his midriff. Only then did he turn the shower off and only then did he catch sight of Alison, Cap's daughter, hosing herself down outside the shower block. She wore a black bikini and was moaning with the cold. Alpine water smashed into her blind face as Tommy ran past her, furiously, and into the safety of the tent.

John had shaken off his lethargy and moseyed off to sniff out breakfast. Cautiously, Tommy sat on his sleeping bag and unpeeled the towelling. He gazed down. There was still minor cause for embarrassment but the heat of

25

the moment was past. It was like a pressure cooker fizzing away on the stove, fit to blow, until somebody slaps the stopper on. How come, Tommy pondered, half of me feels so guilty about this and half of me feels so good?

The expedition rolled off early the next morning, Haggis opting to reach Yugoslavia via Italy, rather than risking the Bedford's brakes on the looming inclines of the Austrian Tyrol. Tommy found himself wedged between Poppy's two young pups from University, both of whom were called Nick. One had the physique and appearance of a very fit bouncer, the other was small, bearded and demonic-looking. Effortlessly, Haggis had christened them Big Nick and Old Nick.

Old Nick had been blessed with a bizarre set of relations. His father had made a startling transition from SAS commander to parish priest. His brother had lived in Basle, eking a living as a freelance baroque trumpeter. Offers of work had not exactly flooded in and, shortly after taking up residence, the young musician had found himself penniless. His only assets were the baroque trumpet and a push bike. The obvious strategy for someone with an English mentality was to leave these objects outside the railway station and wait for an athletic baroque trumpet thief to steal them. A heftily-padded insurance claim could then be submitted and there would once again be money to pay the rent. For three days the bike and trumpet remained propped against the station wall, a brazen invitation to thievery. No-one touched them. 'Wouldn't happen in Wolverhampton,' Old Nick sighed, lamenting the dishonesty of his father's current flock.

3

BALKAN BEACHES

Haggis pulled over outside the gruesomely-named Camping Bled, a delightful site bordered by impressive crags on three sides and on the fourth by a still, clear lake. A white, pebbly beach, gleaming like a boneyard, led down to the water. Within a few hundred strokes of its edge, Tommy could see small islands, clumped by vegetation and boasting fairy castles whose towers thrust gloriously through the greenery.

As the Bedford snorted on beyond the registration barrier, the camp's easy-going atmosphere evaporated. The place bristled. For the spot was a popular one with Yugoslavs taking their well-earned breaks from the tractor factories and spaces were few. No-one warmed to the idea of sharing plots with a score of louse-infested, drunken spoilers from the West. Wherever Haggis eased up, he met a welcoming party of sour faces and leathery hands waving him onwards.

As they headed south, hectares of monotonous maize succeeded each other, broken occasionally by strips of sunflowers. Peasants with brown, creased faces and hats perched at an angle considered jaunty tended them.

Camp sites were non-existent. For two nights running, the truck pulled off onto rubbish tips masquerading as picnic areas. Dented yellow oildrums spilled over with waspy garbage. Rats ran joyously through channels of discarded plastic. They had been eating areas once, hardwood tables and benches with concrete supports, enough to seat a vicar's tea party. Save for a solitary smashed plank, the hardwood had long gone, leaving dozens of stunted protuberances rearing from the litter.

Partly to beat away the rats, the group built a huge bonfire that night. Werner Bolsterley, the portly Swiss, held the stage, lamenting the loss of wildlife since his last visit.

'Before, even ten years ago, everywhere there was birds. Those birds which go flap, flap, flap and bring babies. Now, how many you see? One, maybe two.'

Tommy turned aside to his mum, to find her deep in conversation with Cap. The Captain had spent nine years as a district officer in Papua New Guinea and the night marked the anniversary of his departure. For a tough guy, he could wax nostalgic.

'Seven hundred languages on that island, Pop, including one that's spoken by only thirty four people. Forty thousand inhabitants to see to and only one other bugger that spoke English.'

That was where Cap had contracted malaria. Tommy decided to remove PNG from his mum's hitlist and tripped off to bed, kicking at a squeaking pile of garbage as he crawled in.

John, lethargically christened Blondie that day, had beaten him to it and was, as usual, devouring the contents of a medical encyclopaedia by torchlight. One of the adventurers' great passions on the road was to play Dial-a-Disease. You yelled out a number in turn, anything up to twelve hundred, for it was a thick book, and Blondie turned to the relevant page and described the disease. The direst, the most hideously crippling, was the winner.

Tommy, to his consternation, had been outright

winner three times running. He was not an unduly superstitious kid but it had nevertheless alarmed him that his three choices all involved the passing on of dread diseases by dogs, foxes and wolverines. Since the age of five, he had suffered cynophobia and it was only recently that he could be induced to cross the path of a cocker spaniel. Only chihuahuas held no fear for him. Significantly, his last choice had been rabies and Tommy felt filled with supernatural unease.

As he and Blondie lay there, now in darkness, the conversation moved on to medical euphemisms. Tommy had once heard a doctor on television authorise a BTK in front of an hysterical patient. This had struck him as far more sensitive than blurting out. 'Take him off below the knee, nurse.' Blondie knew lots of these, ranging from SOB, (Short of Breath) to GLM (Good Looking Mum). An equally popular one for those children who are clearly sixpence ha'penny short of a bob but who defy medical analysis was FLK (Funny Looking Kid) although Blondie's favourite turned out to be IWB. This had been the invention of a brassy Aussie on loan to a psychiatric unit.

'IWB, what's that, then?' Tommy questioned, squirming in his sleeping-bag with expectancy.

Blondie harrumphed loudly into the darkness.

'Intercourse With Biscuits.'

Tommy stopped waggling for a moment and concentrated into the gloom. 'What? I don't get it.'

Blondie toyed with the delivery of an adult punchline and then changed his mind. 'I'll tell you when you're older, kid. G'night.'

He swung his back into Tommy's face, crashed his head against the pillow and fell instantly asleep. 'When I'm older,' Tommy thought. 'How many times have I heard that before? When I'm older. What are they trying to protect me from? Does something magical happen to you at eighteen that makes you suddenly able to cope with booze and sex and life and death?' Tommy's thoughts drifted to Flegg's older brother who had hanged himself in his bedroom doorway at twenty three. He thought of Poppy and his dad who still couldn't introduce Jim into a conversation without shedding a tear. Hell, a kid dies two decades ago and they still blubber about him.

Events of the last few days washed about his head as Tommy fell into sleep. Scheisskopf, that's what the woman at the service station had called Pinny. Shithead. It was odd how kids, when they got together from different countries, had conversations that centred around three things: music, football and swear words. They swapped them before they swapped addresses. Scheisskopf. Tommy smiled and gave himself up to sleep.

Blondie's medical knowledge was tested to the full the following day, shortly after the border crossing into Greece. A westbound Mercedes, clogged with Krauts, had had a blow-out at high speed. It had slewed across the lane, swerved aside from oncoming traffic and ploughed through two concrete lamp posts. The corpses of two adults lay strewn across the asphalt, as though inexpertly gutted, and that of a small child lay tossed like a discarded doll in the gutter.

It had just happened. Haggis pulled over some forty metres on, allowing Blondie and the medics time to leap out. They were faced with the prospect of patching gaping wounds with Elastoplast. The three bodies on public display were already beyond all help but close to the car two others lay dying. Tommy and the adventurers stood, helpless, at a respectful distance.

Not so the locals. Cars triple-parked along the highway

in both directions, blocking the progress of the rescue services. From across the fields, peasants gathered up their skirts and ran to the scene, staring open-mouthed at the punctured corpses as kids might at their first matinée. They were close enough to see the flies settle.

Salonika's ambulance arrived forty five minutes later. It had reserved space only for the living; the dead were left by the roadside. Blondie and his team shuffled back, ashen-faced. Cap's wife, Jenny, had already prepared a bucket of water with which to swab their hands. In the event, it took three pails to staunch the flow of redness from their arms. Blondie, in particular, had been sticky to the elbow.

A large sign obscured much of the adventurers' view east. It bore a message for departing holidaymakers and must have been read by the Germans seconds before the blow-out. As the truck trundled up to and beyond it, Tommy and the adventurers turned to read the legend: THANK YOU FOR VISITING GREECE. HAVE A SAFE JOURNEY HOME. One of the sensitive English girls, Books, the librarian from Leicester, threw her face forward and sobbed. Blondie's more volcanic reaction was to lurch down the truck's gangway, grip both the end rails and vomit onto the windscreen of the Peugeot tagging on to their tailboard. Nobody smiled, least of all the Peugeot driver.

By the following night, spirits had revived somewhat, it being Haggis's birthday. The group settled down by the sea at Camping Artemis and it was Tommy's turn to cook. Beer and baklava seemed an obvious choice for a Greek party. With Books in tow, Tommy set out for the nearby town, flipping through her English/Greek diction-ary for 'candles'.

From all points of view, the evening was a resounding success. Away from Poppy's maternal eye, Tommy had

31

managed to down three beakers of wine and, from where he was gyrating, life looked great. Blurred a little, maybe, but inviting. Definitely inviting. The camp site owner and his wife laid on a spot of Greek dancing, on an illuminated square adjacent to their taverna. Although no dance floor Romeo, Tommy surprised himself by coping quite easily with the basic steps. This was something of a shock because back home he was well known for his failure to clap in time to primitive football rhythms on the terraces. Even Miss Brown despaired at the twice-weekly thrashings he gave her piano – a word she told him, curiously enough, that means 'soft' in Italian. However, this Greek dancing lark proved well within his capability. Indeed, it seemed to Tommy that the more he drank, the better he got. Start with the RIGHT, move THREE paces RIGHT and KICK; move LEFT, and KICK on the SECOND. And then, there stood Alison.

She wore a gathered peasant blouse, white, and a pair of sawn-off Levis.

'I thought you were never goin' to ask me to dance, so I thought I'd better ask you.'

She took Tommy's limp hands in hers and moved into the light.

'Do you want to go for a walk now?'

Mostly, the adults had drifted away but there was still a dozen or so diehards on the razzle.

'Tommy, do you want to go for a walk with me?'

They turned the corner of the taverna towards the tents.

'Dad's from Melbourne,' she intoned, pronouncing it 'Mailbin', as was the custom, 'but he moved up to Koonoomoo before I was born.'

They wove between the tents, illuminated by an almost full golden moon and the occasional arc of a pocket torch.

'He's a supermarket manager now,' she continued, slipping her hand up to Tommy's shoulders, 'but he's hoping to give it up to grow strawberries.'

Marc-Marc had pitched his tent at some distance from the encampment, an unusual break with procedure on grounds of security and communication and now they were about ten metres from it. A low, insistent breathing caught their attention as they approached. Instinctively, they quietened, sensing trouble. The breathing quickened, becoming louder and more rhythmical. The narrow sides of the tent billowed and puffed, as if they too were caught up in whatever it was.

'Do you think Marc's okay?' Tommy turned, his face filled with concern. 'It doesn't sound like him. Maybe he needs an inhaler.'

Alison remained stilled in concentration for a few moments longer. Finally, her frown fell away and she relaxed.

'Yeah, I think Marc-Marc's okay. Come on, Tommy, I'll buy you a drink if they're still open.'

She hooked an arm through his in sisterly fashion and they retreated to the square of dancing light. There was a slight breeze now but it failed to convey the words and half-words that broke the silence about Marc's tent.

'Oh, God! Oh, God!'

'Marc! Don't stop, don't stop!'

'Oh, God! Oh, God!'

'Marc!'

'Nokkers!'

4

TURKEY TROT

The haul from the Greek border to Istanbul wasn't unpleasant. Everyone seemed pleased to see them. In Yugoslavia, all the kids had waved as the truck had ground past. In Greece, the adults had lent an occasional hand. But here, the entire populace went berserk. They tore out of houses, across fields, to wave and yell like demons. Little boys rammed fingers in their mouths at improbable angles and shrieked 'FWIT FWIT FWIT FWIT'. This astonishing fwitting could be heard above the engine's roar at a distance of several hundred metres.

Food was plentiful. Carts were dotted periodically along the excellent roads, piled high with melons and marrows. Each cart boasted maybe half a thousand fruits. At one point, Tommy counted ten adjacently-parked melon carts. That meant a lot of melons. Beyond the wayside produce, maize grew and sunflowers sprouted. Tommy had the feeling that it was all more orderly than in Greece. The impression lasted until the truck wheezed into Londra Camping, on the western edge of Istanbul. 'This is it,' Haggis sneered, 'the end of civilisation as we know it.'

The city that has outlawed sleep, Poppy thought poetically. City of dolmuses and handcarts, cacophonous horns and minarets. City of stiff, dusty beggars and urchins playing down cobbled alleyways until well beyond midnight. City of spitters and hawkers, screamers and roarers. And above all, whether at bruised sunset or grey dawn, city of St Sophia and Sultanachmed whose imposing silhouettes rise as sentinels over the rabble below.

With a jolt, Tommy realised that he wouldn't be sleeping under canvas that night. Or the next. He watched Blondie struggling with the flysheet before dropping down to help. Dad, who seemed a long way distant now, like some faded photograph from the past, had befriended an Istanbuli engineer whose ship had been in dry dock for repair. Their correspondence and friendship had continued over the years though they'd met just the once. When he'd had a telephone installed, Mustafa's first call was to Manchester. When he discovered Jog's son worshipped soccer, he'd despatched framed photographs of both Besiktas and Galatasaray, Istanbul's footballing envoys to the world.

Ten minutes later, Mustafa's car drew up. It was a '62 Ford, roomy, and with a magnificent collection of dents. The welcoming party was seven strong and there still seemed ample room for Poppy and Tommy.

Mustafa's apartment was in Besiktas, only a shout away from the ground. In seconds, Poppy had been spirited away with the women in the direction of the kitchen, leaving Mustafa, his brother-in-law Ferruh and Tommy to mull over old photographs and letters.

'What is this?' queried Mustafa, as Tommy stretched to catch an elusive print, slipping to the linoleum. He touched lightly beneath Tommy's T-shirt, at a wrap of fabric gathered stickily about his midriff. 'Are you carrying a gun? Perhaps you are protecting your mother from Turkish bandits?' He smiled.

'No. It's me moneybelt. Mum made it.' Tommy gratefully unswathed the white, zippered wrap, grubby now from sweat. 'It's got $200 inside. I even keep it on at night.'

'Well,' Ferruh replied, smiling warmly, 'you can take it off now. There are no thieves here.' Uncertainly, Tommy gazed outside the room's four open windows and listened to the clamour as it crept up from the street and over the sills. His smile looked unconvincing as he dumped his spends for the next three months onto the dubious safety of Mustafa's table.

And then the food appeared. Pasta and parsley soup, aubergines, onions and tomatoes, green beans in sauce, salad with coriander. Politely, Poppy tried to learn the Turkish names but by the time she had wrapped her tongue around 'seriye corbasi' they had been swept downstairs and into the car. It was sightseeing time, with Sultanachmed as top priority.

The Blue Mosque appealed to all Poppy's senses save that of smell. Its tiled dome and seven minarets would arouse noble feelings in even the most heartless, with the possible exceptions, her son argued, of Manchester City supporters. And American tourists. As Poppy and Tommy cut a swathe through the cheesy whiff, they ghosted past an obese team from smalltown USA, all tequila T-shirts and swinging Canons. Hubby attempted a rare moment's private communion with the cool beauty of Sultanachmed but his monstrous wife had her fatty eyes on the watch.

'C'mon, George. How do you expect to see Asia in three weeks if you keep stopping to look at things?'

The party continued the next day, touring beyond Taksim and up to Camlica Tepesi. Istanbul's highest spot was topped by a spacious tearoom and encircled by a drive for horse-drawn carriages. Each vehicle, ornately fitted, contained a proud, tear-stained mum and a pert, well-turned-out little boy of ten or eleven. Poppy was fascinated.

'What's going on here, Mustafa?'

Mustafa nodded solemnly. 'They are going to have their pennies halved.'

Poppy mulled over the possible interpretations then tried again. 'I don't understand. Who is doing what?'

'The little boys. They are going to have their pennies halved.'

It took two forays into the dictionary to clarify matters. Mustafa's first error was really a matter of mispronunciation. He should have said 'penises'. The second mistake was more mathematical. Having their penises halved was altogether too drastic a calculation. They were there merely for circumcision.

Ferruh's wife was called Hilkat and she told fortunes. No Tarot pack or crystal ball for her. She specialised in coffee grounds. In one deft exercise after breakfast, she'd inverted Tommy's coffee cup, clamped it to the saucer and returned it to its original position before he could say 'Nescafe'. Mysteriously, the grounds had arranged themselves into kaleidoscopic patterns and it was on these that Hilkat was focusing her attention. She was engaged in the Turkish equivalent of reading the tea-leaves.

'I can see three long journeys ahead of you. I see three people watching. They have great care for you. Beware of water.'

If Hilkat's opening statements had been met by mild amusement, her next made Tommy stiffen.

'There is an animal that is not pleasing to you. This animal has a big sickness. There is great danger. You must not let this animal touch you.'

'What is it? Do you know its name?' Tommy was affecting nonchalance but his knuckles were white.

'I do not know the word in English. In French it is "le chien".'

By the time Mustafa had returned with Poppy from the souk, laden with spices for the truck, Tommy had recovered his composure. He sat patiently explaining a joke to Ferruh.

'So this bloke is walking past a scrapyard when an old banger dislodges from the top of the pile and falls on his leg.' Ferruh nodded. 'It tears it off almost, it's hanging by a thread. The bloke, a Manchester City fan, is lying there on the pavement, trying to tie it back on again with his scarf when a genie appears.'

'Please,' interposed Mustafa, caught up now in Tommy's vivid little drama, 'what is this "genie"?'

'You should know!' snorted Tommy, though not rudely. 'Aladdin and his magic lamp. Whooooo!' He gave a passing demonstration of a powerful genie extracting itself from Mustafa's coffee pot. Mustafa nodded, as if all was now clear.

'So the genie says, "I am the genie of the scrapyard and I can grant you one wish." He looks down at the bloke on the pavement juggling with his leg and says, "So, wish."

'"I wish . . . I wish," the City fan says, "I wish I could have me leg fixed on again." The genie bends down and examines the injury. It's no good. He can almost pick the leg up in his hands and float off with it.

'"Sorry, mate,", the genie says. "Can't do that. Too far gone."'

From the kitchen, Hayat, Mustafa's wife and Hilkat the fortune-teller slipped in to catch the mounting excitement.

'"Make another wish," he says. "Anything you like. I promise you your will shall be obeyed." The bloke thinks for a moment then puts it to the genie.

'"Okay," he says, "I'd like City to win the league this year. And, wait a minute, the cup as well. Yeah, that's it.

I'd like City to do the double." The genie goes all sort of embarrassed and starts to edge away, like, back into the scrapyard. "Ere, hang on," the bloke says, "yer said anything, didn't yer?"

'The genie looks sort of shifty and won't look him in the eye.

'"Tell you what," he says eventually. "Let's have another look at that leg."'

Tommy burst out laughing for them, as a signal that the joke was over. But the niceties of soccer rivalry in Manchester were lost on them and the best they could do was slap his back and smile. Later, in the car, heading back for Camping Londra, Tommy considered whether the joke would have worked in translation, substituting Besiktas and Galatasaray. He vowed, as sad farewells were made, to tell it in Turkish at their next reunion.

'Take a walk on the wild side?' Haggis observed, as Poppy and Tommy slung their bags back on the truck. 'I told you it was the end of civilisation as we know it.'

'I reckon it was the start of civilisation when we crossed the Channel,' Nokkers joked, 'away from all you bloody Poms!'

Tommy reflected for a moment on Rolf's generosity to complete strangers back in Salzburg, on the spontaneity and laughter at Camping Artemis and now at Mustafa's great-heartedness. Nokkers might have been joking but there was an element of truth in the comment somewhere.

The road to Gallipoli involved a bit of backtracking but once the truck had veered south onto the peninsula, the scenery changed. Undulating, forested landscape replaced the parched cultivated vistas alongside the border road. Tiny tots and women stood in isolated clearings, tending sorry herds of goats.

The Australians were keen to visit Lone Pine memorial.

The Gallipoli campaign of World War I had led to the loss of 36,000 Commonwealth lives, Cap had informed Tommy, of which 1,167 fell at Lone Pine. The area had been overrun in the initial Anzac landing and then re-taken by the Turks on the evening of the following day. It was then fortified to become one of the most heavily defended in the Turkish line. Despite this, a frenzied Allied assault led to its capture on 6th August, 1915. It had then been held until the final evacuation.

'The bastards left the bodies out to rot in the sun,' Cap continued. 'They didn't have the decency to bury 'em. Our lads came back in 1918 and they were still there, all black and stinking. That was their first job,' he choked, nodding away a forgivable tear, 'to get out the spades and bury 'em.'

What amazed Poppy was the tender age at which these young men fell, leaving their cattle lands and crops and glorious sunsets in Australia to be slaughtered before they reached twenty. She stopped to pay her respects at the headstones of two of the maturer men:

388 sergeant
A. W. THUNDER
6th BN. AUSTRALIAN INF.
25th. April, 1915, age 23
DUTY BRAVELY DONE

BELIEVED TO BE
BURIED IN THIS CEMETERY
SECOND LIEUTENANT
C. W. WHIDBORNE
4TH. BN. AUSTRALIAN INF.
6/9TH AUGUST, 1915, AGE 33
HE HAS OUTSOARED
THE SHADOW OF OUR NIGHT

Snorting back tears, she turned to find Haggis by her side, reading the same epitaphs. After a long silence, unusual for the Scotsman, he turned to Poppy, burning with anger. 'Well, I know what I'd have wanted them to put on my grave.' He paused to gaze at the straggly lines of pine and untilled land that led down to a nondescript beach. 'Died pointlessly.'

Subdued somewhat, the adventurers pushed on in the direction of Cannakale, port of embarkation for the Dardenelles and Asia. They stopped short of the town in a clearing for lunch, liked the look of the place and decided to overnight there. Tents thudded from the cab roof as Cap lit a campfire.

The smoke attracted human flotsam in the way that a butcher's shop attracts dogs. Within minutes of the first grey plumes billowing upwards in a windless sky, a rash of ragged and disfigured specimens had surrounded the truck. They pressed with mouths agape. Fearfully, the prim English girls scraped together their scattered possessions, secured them in locked tents and then stood po-faced on guard, arms at the fold and ready for nonsense.

Tommy's gipsies failed to notice. With a cry, they fell forward, proffering gifts of fruit and buckets of tomatoes at the fazed travellers. Intuitively, they acknowledged Haggis as the headman and without protest he was dragged to a much-needed source of fresh water. Tommy dwelt on the possibilities of such hospitality being extended to itinerants at home. The last time a Romany encampment had set up on wasteland on the outskirts of town, the yobbos from the local council estate had gone in at midnight with petrol bombs.

Tommy, like the Australians, didn't find the classical sites of Turkey that appealing. He preferred being on the beach, watching Werner or Cap barbecuing, or kicking a football around with Marc-Marc and the two Nicks. To his

41

surprise, the theatre at Ephesus wasn't half bad.

'See this place, Tommy,' Werner muttered in an undertone, as if he were betraying state secrets. 'Guess how many they packed in? 24,000. Know how many lived in the city? 300,000. Know how old it is? 2000 years.' Tommy could only compare in terms of soccer grounds but Werner led him on. 'Did you know, Tommy, that the acoustics in this place were so perfect that a coin dropped centre stage could be heard hitting the ground anywhere in the auditorium. Listen.'

It was as if the French tour guide far below had been eavesdropping on their conversation. Tommy and Werner were centrally seated, on the highest possible bank of seats. Down below, the Frenchman held one arm imperiously aloft, trying in vain to capture the attention of his indifferent charges, and let a coin fall. After an interval of what seemed like two or three seconds, the sound of its tinkling on the stone flags reached the adventurers perched on the top tier.

Later, the group cut inland to bathe in the hot springs of Pammukale. The most enticing thing about the place was its name in translation, Cotton Castle. Its white, petrified cascade looked impressive enough with its naturally formed tubs of spring water but Tommy found paddling was like slipping one's feet into warm, wet putty. He felt much happier heading over the hill to the necropolis, the Roman graveyard where they were to encamp.

The place itself looked brimful of spooks. Out on a hilltop, the site stretched over several barren acres. Unmistakeably, it was a city of the dead, littered with discoloured tombs and rotting vaults, the darkened home of snakes and scorpions. At a distance, dogs bayed, as if waiting for nightfall to continue their 2000-year-old feast on decomposing corpses. As thunderclouds congregated above, a sudden wind buffeted the encampment.

'I think I'll stay in the truck tonight, Haggis,' Sally announced. 'Wouldn't want to blow away.'

'You can always join us under the truck,' Blondie ventured. Of late, he'd taken to flattening a groundsheet beneath the stars, in the shadow of the Bedford. Nokkers had joined him once or twice. Tommy couldn't work out whether it was his 'Doctor, Doctor' jokes Blondie was seeking to avoid or whether he was hatching plans to plonk more than his stethoscope on Nokkers' national monuments. Consequently, Tommy had erected his tent alone, siting it a measure apart from the others, for no particular reason.

As dusk fell, they sensed the chill presence of the dead. The wind lowed through arches of collapsed stone and spirit dogs bayed increasingly at the whiff of pilchards drifting tantalisingly over the graves. The encircling tombs exuded disapproval at this intrusion of their silent and deserted state. The light played strange and terrifying tricks, driving an increasing number of adventurers to the sanctuary of their canvas as the shadows lengthened.

It was time, Tommy decided, for his best ghost stories, drawn principally from Leroy, his mucker at scout camp. Leroy lived next door to Rosetta, a spiritualist, in Moss Side and, boy, did she have tales to tell. Tommy kicked in the embers of the camp fire, sending sparks scudding across the twilight, and then embraced the darkness of their imaginations. Sally had stayed up, as had Books, Pinny and Marc-Marc. Nokkers and Blondie had turned in, beside the truck, but they were still slobbing around, half-listening.

He opened with one of his best shots, personalising all the fine details of Rosetta's clients.

'I only saw my grandpa once,' he began, 'and that was eighteen years after he died.' Tommy raked his eyes about the circle and saw that he'd got them hooked. 'Grandma kept the house on though she didn't need the room. The family had all gone by then.' The knot of adventurers moved in more tightly, as the howling of the invisible hounds became as one with the wind. 'I think she kept it on as a memorial to him. She never changed his bedroom once she'd lost him. Not even the sheets. Kept it just the way it was. Like a shrine.' Tommy paused for effect, pulling at a mug of coffee. 'She'd moved downstairs straight afterwards, what with her wonky legs and all. It was one thing less to worry about. Upstairs, it was like stepping back in time. Not centuries like, but a generation. The furniture was all cheap and brown. Me mam says it was all you could get just after the war. The mirrors were all bolted on, they didn't have frames. One on the dresser, one on the wardrobe. The light shade was all tassely, like you see hanging down over snooker tables sometimes.'

'This kid's gonna be an interior decorator,' Nokkers contributed, drawing on a cigarette as she gazed up to the heavens. 'Go on, Tommy, go for it.'

'I wasn't banned from the room exactly but I knew Gran didn't really like me being there. She was always around when I was, watching me like a museum guide. I don't know what she thought I was going to do.

'Anyway, one Friday in December, me mum and dad have a Christmas party on at work and they can't get a babysitter. Everyone's out getting smashed, 'cos it's the Friday between Christmas Day and New Year. I'm eight. Gran isn't feeling so good, not good enough to cross town to look after me anyway, so I get packed off there.'

Poppy materialised out of the gloaming, causing Books' heart to flutter at her silent approach.

'Look at that sky. Beautiful. It's going to be a wonderful day tomorrow.' She cupped her coffee between her palms and smiled fondly. 'Tommy, don't you get bothering people.'

'He's just fine, Poppy. No worries.'

'I'll bid you all goodnight then. Goodnight, everybody.'

'Night, Poppy.'

'Night, Mum.'

Tommy held off for a second. He didn't want any further interruptions, especially as his tale picked up the pace.

'We talk a little and we watch television. Gran still had an old black-and-white set but I don't think she could see so good anyway so there wasn't a lot of point her changing. Finally, she makes me a cocoa and shuffles off to the next room. I sit around for a while, thinking about the morning. United are away at Southampton and the supporters' coach leaves early on. I finish my drink and I'm just about to make my way upstairs when there's a power cut. Bingo. Everything goes out. Lights in the lounge, the hall, the staircase. I whisper for Gran because she might have candles but she's dead to the world. So, upstairs I go, making my way to the guest room, thinking that I've got a pretty neat excuse for not taking a wash.'

'Hey, look at that!' Blondie yells. 'A shooting star!' Whether it's his yell or the star that does it, the howling from the perimeter of the encampment intensifies.

'Anyways, I'm dog tired . . .'

'Not like those bar-stards,' growled Nokkers, hurling a rock into the void.

'. . . and I push open the nearest door and just flake out on the bed. Don't even take my clothes off. After a while, it gets a little chilly. It wakes me and I sort of drag my clothes off in the dark and slip between the sheets. I guess I was just about to give up the ghost when this light starts flashing from inside the room. I'm drowsy and a little confused and I think maybe the electric's back on. I haul myself around, pull my eyes open and there's this little blue flash spinning round the room. Like a spark. Electrical fault, I think. I know I'm only eight but I'm a smart kid. I begin to gather my senses. Only it's brighter now and I can start to pick out furniture inside the room. First the outlines, then the details. And it hits me. I'm in the wrong room. I'm in Grandpa's room.'

A low moaning began from the entrance of the vault nearest the encampment. It was an arrangement of bare stone blocks, slightly higher than a man, wider than the span of his arms and as deep and it had lasted two thousand years. By day, had you taken a photograph, it would have been an indifferent grey but in the moonlight, it glowed silver. Guarding its entrance were two upright slabs with a horizontal stone at chest height. In between, even by day, briars ran like wire and darkness fell. Whether the lowing was the moaning of a young dog or the wind playing tricks or something else was open to conjecture, but none of the adventurers wished to find out at that moment.

'It's light enough to make things out now. Not everywhere. The corners are still in deep shadow and there are, like, patches of the room that are lighter than others. It's a strange sort of light. Not natural, not artificial, but I'm reaching out to my left to flick on the bedside lamp. No-one's used it for eighteen years and I'm just hoping it's still okay.' Tommy permitted himself a thin smile. 'Gran was always telling me how they built things to last in those days. So I'm stretching out, clawing for the switch, when I suddenly catch a glimpse in the mirror. It's on the dressing table, facing the bed, reflecting the bottom half.'

'Boy, do I get the impression you've told this before!' Nokkers snorted, pulling a sleeping-sheet over her shoulders.

'And I can see this man, in the reflection, sitting on the edge of the bed, looking up towards me.' Tommy held his breath for an instant. 'He's old and tired looking but he's kind of smiling. He's got one of those old-fashioned shirts without a collar and red braces. His face is all grizzled and you knew his bosses had worked him to death over the years. He's familiar somehow but I just can't place him and, this is really strange, my heart's pounding but I'm not that scared. It's, like, scary but I know he's not going to rip my throat out. There's waves of kindness and sadness, all mixed up, coming from him. So . . .' Tommy pulled himself upright and threw the dregs of his coffee in the fire. 'I bit my bottom lip really hard, like I do when we've conceded a penalty, and I drag my eyes round to the foot of the bed. That was a bit like a Reds' penalty as well. You want to look but you don't want to look. My head goes round in slow motion till I'm nearly there, than I snap it round suddenly . . .'

There was total silence on the site now. There had been a lull in the wind, the hounds on the perimeter had relented momentarily and there was not a twitch from the adventurers, even Nokkers.

'. . . and I'm alone. There's no-one in the room. I flash back to the mirror. Nothing. Back to the bed. Nothing. I grab the bedside lamp, fumble with the switch 'cos my heart's going like a piston now, and there . . . there on the bed is an indentation of where the old guy was sitting. It's like there's an obstruction in my throat now. I want to call out for Gran but all the air passages have gone sticky and clogged up. I can't even find any air to breath out. So I kick down at the indentation, thinking that I'm under some spell and if I can only get rid of this I'll be freed. But it won't move. I push my feet down to where it starts . . . and they won't go any further. I couldn't see him but he was still there.'

A rash of shooting stars broke across the sky but they passed without comment.

'I was choking with fear. I tipped out of bed on the other side, slipped on the rug, scrambled up and fled from the room.' Tommy shivered. 'It still gives me a chill to think about it. The lock on the door was one of those old brass gadgets where you slide a button to the left to lock it. I was dead sure it wasn't going to open.'

'So where was your gran?' Books' large brown eyes and ugly spectacles made her look more owlish than ever in the moonlight.

'Downstairs still. I went bowling down and fell in a heap at the bottom. Even when she picked me up, I was still choking and couldn't speak.'

'So this old guy,' Pinny posed, never having been particularly quick on the uptake, 'I suppose was your grinpa?'

Tommy nodded. 'I'd seen a few photographs already, like. Gran always had a couple round the house. But he'd be dolled up for something, you know, a wedding or special occasion. I didn't recognise him in his working gear. Gran pulled out a few snaps the next day. She'd taken them in the back garden, the day after he retired.'

'And was it him?' Sally questioned, although Tommy's sincerity had burned through his story like a slow fuse and she already knew the answer.

'Oh, it was him all right. G'night.' Tommy stooped to place his mug on the charred grass and turned forlornly into the moonlight. He traipsed off, head hanging, until he was reasonably secure that he was out of earshot. Leroy had told the tale at Whitsun camp. Three months and he hadn't forgotten a detail. Leroy would have been proud.

'YEE-SSSSS!' Tommy whooped up into the air,

kicking the heels of his trainers behind him. If it had been Old Trafford, he'd have sprung to the ground, double-somersaulted and held his arms aloft to receive the crushing adulation of his team-mates.

It was a moment to savour but it didn't last. By the time Tommy had unzipped his tent and thrown his sleeping bag over his shoulders, the triumph had passed. There was total darkness now in the necropolis. They must have kicked the fire out before turning in and it had made the dogs bold. And, significantly, he was alone. Tommy, never one to be short of strategies, calculated that if he stayed dressed, and if he kept his Swiss knife handy, and if he ran fast, he could be back on board in about fifteen seconds from the moment of unzipping the tent.

Half an hour passed. The noise outside had become deafening. Suddenly, there was a terrifying new development and Tommy jerked up, stricken with fear. Surely, that had been the sound of dogs padding about inside the encampment. Tins clattered. There had been no time to bury the evening's refuse and unmistakeably the hounds were now wedging their rabid noses into jagged tins of pilchards.

Without warning, a quarrel broke out. A young pup appeared to have strayed into the encampment, an intruder who began piercing the night air with a wild, unbroken series of yelps. It was unearthly. Tommy had never heard a creature sound like this and he felt pretty sure he knew what it was. Rabies. *La rage.* The scavenging pack seemed to know it too. In a frenzy, they set about the pup, putting the pilchards on one side for a moment in order to rip it to shreds. The most horrifying cacophony ensued. Behind the limp security of his canvas walls, Tommy quaked.

And then he heard Nokkers. The battle had seemingly spilt over to the truck area, embroiling the trapped

Nokkers in its madness. She was going berserk, as if demented beasts were rending the flesh from her rolling body in juicy, jagged strips.

'Aaagh! Geddof yer bar-stard!' That was Blondie. They were eating his face. Inside the tent, Tommy was fumbling with his pocket knife with urgency, hands trembling at the pandemonium outside.

And then he heard feet pounding in his direction. It was Nokkers. From all around her came the sound of biting, snapping dogs.

'Tommy! Tommy! Open up, for God's sake! Let me in! Aaaaagh!' Her shrill scream tore through the night at yet another fleshy wound. She pulled wildly at his tent door. 'Tomm . . my! Aaaaagh!' Her final words were lost beneath a great, concerted roar from the hounds and a gargled sob from Nokkers. He guessed they'd got her throat.

Tommy became demented. His childhood fears, his ill-luck at Dial-a-Disease and Hilkat's dark predictions had all be leading to this moment. His body shook uncontrollably and he felt faint. This was the moment he'd been warned against. And in his thirteenth year. He should have known. If he opened the door now . . . 'I can't, I can't!' Tommy collapsed in a pile, sobbing.

Abruptly, the tugging on his tent door stopped. All extraneous noise ceased. At a stroke, the campsite had been reduced to total silence. There were no further screams and no sounds of dogs. Tommy raised his head in disbelief. Was it a miracle?

Shaking somewhat less, but with every muscle still tense, Tommy cocked an ear and listened. It was true that he could hear hounds baying but only faintly. They were the ones he had heard on arrival. They must have been a quarter of a mile away. Here, on the site, there was nothing.

'Nokkers! Nokkers!' Tommy still dare not move but the continued silence reassured him. 'Nokkers! Are you all right?' Warily, he leaned forward, his hand on the zipper. 'Nokkers?' Still nothing. Inch by desperate inch, Tommy nervously established contact with the outside world. It was as if he were unpicking each tooth separately. When the gap was wide enough to peer through, he extended his head until his nostrils hung outside the canvas. Nothing. There were no lights, no prowling hounds and no piles of raw flesh outside his tent. What in God's name had happened? Had the dead resented this intrusion into their burial ground and sent in their hell-hounds to wreak vengeance? Tommy became consumed with supernatural dread. Was he the lone survivor?

Bravely, he ripped open the remaining stretch of his zip and plunged into the darkness. As if on cue, a huge ironic cheer ballooned to his right and the flashes of twenty cameras popped. The entire group were ensconced, as if arranged for a family photograph.

'How ya doin', hero?' yelled Nokkers.

'Woof! Woof! Woof!' barked Haggis.

'How-oooooh!' wailed Blondie, the rabid pup.

'That'll teach you to scare people!' Poppy laughed, with just an edge of concern in her voice.

It was left to Haggis to round off the evening's entertainment. 'Let's have three cheers for Tommy,' he roared, 'Tommy the Tiger! Hip, hip . . .'

Camping Deniz, the adventurers' next major stop, was a crescent of white sand set alongside the turquoise waters of the Aegean, a few kilometres from Fethiye. Hills rolled in the background and the sun bore down all day long from a cloudless sky. Two or three restaurants nestled discreetly in the palm groves, perfect for romantic têtes-à-têtes. Offshore, a yacht lay anchored and, beyond it, Rhodes beckoned.

51

Tommy spent most of his time snorkelling or coaching Marc-Marc in the arts of the penalty shoot-out whilst, behind them, relationships blossomed. Poppy, never one to be nosey, had nevertheless been amongst the first to pick up on Old Nick, the theology student, and Miss Swiss, the coy young lady from Berne.

Poppy had been spending much of her free time sketching and, shortly after lunch on the Saturday, she caught them strolling across her vista and heading for the woods, ostensibly to pick wild flowers. Spot, the camp site's resident pooch, probably attracted by their animal heat, had set off in pursuit.

After several hours billing and cooing, during which time Spot received scant attention and the local signposts even less, the couple found themselves irretrievably lost. They stood clueless, hand entwined in hand, by the border of a dusty road and gazed forlornly at the horizon. Spot barked encouragement and was kicked for his pains. And then, by a stroke of that good fortune that so often attends lovers, a rusty cloud rose to their left. A motorised vehicle was weaving towards them, hiccupping round the potholes. The lovers hurrahed. Old Nick squeezed his girl's hand and nipped a kiss on the tip of her nose in relief.

The car drew nearer. It was a taxi. The lovers hurrahed again. Spot raced round in circles. Old Nick made as if to flag the vehicle down but his gesture was unnecessary; it was stopping anyway.

A peasant and his tethered goat leaped out of the back, grinning equally from ear to ear. Incomprehensively, the man was wearing winter woollies and a balaclava. One of them stank, probably the goat.

'Camping Deniz?' Nick enquired of the taxi driver who looked to be bursting with ecstasy.

'Camping Deniz!' he affirmed, almost overcome with

emotion.

'How much?' Nick slid his hand inside his jeans pocket.

'How much?' wept the taxi driver, swinging his car erratically in a half circle before blasting off in a fog of red dust. A lonely tear trickled the length of Miss Swiss's damask cheek.

'Camping Deniz!' the woolly peasant roared, fetching Old Nick a hefty slap on the back. He marched off exuberantly along the ochred wheel ruts with the two young lovers, the dog and the goat in reluctant tow.

They toiled for half an hour before a second motorised hum caused their hearts to flutter. It came from the same direction as the taxi. The Turk paused to dislodge some of the dust from his boots in anticipation of a free ride. The goat raised its almond eyes to the heavens and methodically began to lick its hooves.

From out of the dust, a moped approached, wobbling under the weight of two more securely wrapped peasants. Nick made to let it pass but his new friend and the goat joined forces to erect a living barricade across its path. With a whine, the moped hove to.

'Camping Deniz!' gesticulated the Turk, rapturously indicating his foot-sore little party.

'Camping Deniz,' the driver nodded, a treacly grin spreading across his face. And so it was that three woolly Turks, Old Nick and Miss Swiss, Spot and the goat teetered back into camp on a two-seater moped. It was seven o'clock by the sun and a substantial barbecue appeared to be under construction.

'Thank God you're here!' Haggis stormed. 'I thought it was going to be pilchards again.' He strode past the confounded lovers and addressed his additional comments to their original woolly friend.

'What!' Miss Swiss's face had lost its original bloom and become pallid. 'Do you mean . . . ? Her voice trailed away as she gazed from the barbecue where Cap was sharpening his butcher's knives to the peasant's winking charge. She swung to remonstrate with an impassive Haggis. 'Are you joking?'

Lazily, he turned a hand towards the Turk. Smiling, the man drew a fluttering finger the length of his throat, winked obscenely at her and spat at the goat.

The lazy perambulation around the Turkish coastline continued the next morning as the adventurers headed for Antalya and beyond. There was no point hurrying for the area's attractions were too good to miss. Clear waters sparkled to their right, bananas, carob and cotton grew to their left. Crusader castles such as Anamur dotted the landscape periodically.

There was more of interest now along the highway. Trucks bearing the legend 'ALLAH KORUSUN' were far more in evidence. Haggis had translated sagely, 'God protect us. And the way they bloody drive, he needs to.' Having observed these portable scrapyards bombing through the gorges, overtaking on blind bends, Tommy chose not to disagree.

Dirty, crop-headed little waifs were another feature these days. They'd pitch themselves on sharp bends dangling plastic bags of peaches and figs. As wagons fighting the gradient slowed to negotiate the curves, these tiny entrepreneurs would race alongside the driver's cab, tempting him with their juiciest fruit. Their barefoot feet would pump along the hot tarmac for several hundred metres. Once a day, perhaps, they made a sale.

At Tarsus, the truck turned inland beyond the Cicilian Gate and into Capadocia, a region of unearthly land-scapes and vast underground metropolises. Derinkuyu, in particular, gripped Tommy. This subterranean wonder, constructed by the Hittites 4000 years ago, was seven levels deep and could at one time have accommodated between 10-20,000 people. Its features included fifty ventilation shafts, wells, churches and wine-brewing areas. It boasted large, circular stones to roll across passageways in the event of attack just, Tommy thought, like those in *Raiders of the Lost Ark*. Astonishingly, Werner told him, this eighth wonder of the world had not been discovered until 1962.

The group's progression into Syria entailed a haul back to Tarsus and on via Antakya. It was a long slog, eating up several days. Coincidentally, wherever the group elected to pitch camp, the gagging smell of decomposing donkey rose to bid them welcome. The first time it had happened, Tommy had sniffed surreptitiously at his armpits before breathing with relief. He caught Alison watching him but she just smiled and blew a kiss. She spent much of her time these days with Young Nick, the crop-haired muscular kid with a flair for statistics. He'd spent his last four years at a southern university handling computers but from the zonked-out expression on Alison's face, the statistics he'd been dealing with of late had been of a softer, more malleable kind altogether.

The group paused for lunch at Iskenderun, the landing place of Alexander the Great. 'Turks say "Iskenderun",' Werner had informed Tommy, 'we say "Alexander".'

'We say "Johann",' Frau Bolsterley added thought-fully, 'and you say "John".'

'The Russians say "Ivan" and . . .' Blondie paused for less than a second but Books had beaten him to it.

'Scandinavians say "Jan".'

'Irish say "Sean",' Old Nick contributed.

'. . . and in France, they say "Jean".'

Tommy broke in. 'In Spain, they say "Juan".'

There was a pause, broken by Poppy. 'Goodness, I didn't realise it was so popular. Whatever do they say in Turkey?'

Haggis ground the truck to an asthmatic halt. Two stone-faced conscripts in olive fatigues approached, each with an automatic rifle clamped across his chest.

'They say, "Get off your backsides and get your passports ready. We're in Syria."'

5

DESERT HIGHWAYS

Haggis fought against the border road for several kilometres, coughing past plantations of young pine and still green lakes. The area was a disputed one and neither Turkey nor Syria felt disposed to make things easy for travellers.

Without warning, the hills gave way to a flat, drab landscape, a parched agricultural plain that had all the attractions of a building site. Breeze blocks clogged isolated melon beds together with decomposing refuse that had drifted away from the towns. The only other presence was that of the military. Anti-aircraft batteries spiked the sky and the towns swarmed with hollow-eyed soldiers on furlough. Inland, the scrubby desert flats buzzed with armies on manoeuvre. There was nothing save for floppy tents and tanks and marching men and sand.

The adventurers camped rough that night, on marshy ground by the roadside, within hailing distance of that bastion of the Crusades, Krak des Chevaliers. Mosquitoes, buzzing like chainsaws, launched a devastating night attack on the party. Rats crept quietly from the fields to forage for droppings, picking between the adventurers' toes for fallen tidbits.

It took Jenny, Cap's wife, to lighten the mood of the dispirited adventurers. A plump and cheery nurse in her early forties, she sat delousing her daughter with an air of unusual concentration. Alison sat wincing as her mum picked and tugged the lice from her hair.

'Oh, they love the night time, fleas,' she sang. 'It's the only time they can relax. All day long, they're having to cling on like grim death. But when we're asleep and not moving, boy, do they have a good time!' As if to illustrate the fact, she made a sudden triumphant lunge at an inhabited area of her daughter's scalp. 'Gotcha! Yer little bagger!'

Jenny went on to explain to an absorbed audience that each female flea mated eight times a night and there are four times as many females as males. Big Nick mulled over these logistics and turned in for the night feeling somewhat inadequate.

Their next port of call was Palmyra, a 'lost city' way out in the wilderness beyond Homs. Seventeen hundred years ago, it had been the proud boast of Queen Zenobia that she would construct a city whose grandeur would rival that of Rome's. Piqued by this, the Romans let her get on with it and then at an opportune moment stepped in for a demolition job. Zenobia herself was lugged to Rome in chains as an example to others who might fancy an architectural fling.

What the Romans had left impressed Tommy. After an eight-hour haul over relentless scrub, the truck suddenly wheezed to a halt in sight of a vast, fertile oasis. To one side lay the town and to the other the remains of Zenobia's vision. Sheltered from public view, the group pitched camp beside the temple of Bel. The logic in this was twofold: it permitted the cooks release from the dry desert wind that would otherwise have seasoned their bolognese, coating it with a sandy Parmesan, and it protected the females aboard from local harassment.

Even a broad like Nokkers found Syria a heavy scene.

Where the women were, no-one knew. Maybe they were all working in ammunition factories, assembling bullets for the front line. On the streets they certainly weren't, for although the pavements teemed with the local populace, they were of one sex only. The adventuresses might well have been the first women the Syrians had seen in weeks.

In the event, by sunset the encampment had been ringed by a posse of barrel-chested lawmen in djellabahs. They wore djellabahs, they said, because they were secret police. No molestation took place. Flanked by security men, the happy band relaxed as the sun, like a fat orange balloon, plopped out of sight behind Hadrian's arch. By morning, the confidence of the single girls had been won over. They gladly consented to take breakfast in the private fruit gardens of those handsome and distinguished custodians of the law.

Poppy too had been swayed by the gravelly tones and gentlemanly bearing of the Chief of Police. Tommy would have joined them but his guts were doing an impression of a non-swimming orchestra playing under-water. He was a sucker for fruit but even he knew that he should have set aside that seventeenth fig. As Poppy left with her sweet-smelling escort, Tommy sank back on the free benches of the truck and slipped his headphones on.

As Poppy wound her way about the cool, canopied passageways of the oasis, she wondered aloud at Nature's cunning.

'It's marvellous! Absolutely marvellous! I mean, how can it be so stifling out there and so cool and pleasant in these gardens? It's incredible!'

The Chief of Police nodded his head slightly in assent and led her on firmly.

His garden was an exotic allotment. Sheltered on all sides by baked walls, it proliferated with lemons, figs and pomegranates. Apart from the narrow wooden door by which they had entered, it was entirely secret and self-contained. Had Poppy had a stool and raised herself on tiptoe, she might possibly have been able to peer into a neighbouring patch. She turned smiling and lamented a lost opportunity.

'Oh, it's wonderful! I wish I'd brought my sketchbook.'

The Chief of Police was kneeling, tugging at a tangled mass of reluctant produce. He rose, with a bloated yellow melon in each hand. He passed one over to Poppy and ran his free hand over its skin, caressing it gently, as one might a lover.

'Are these fruits not fine and ripe?' he growled softly. 'But not as fine and ripe as yours, my pigeon.' He lunged swiftly for Poppy's breasts, cupping one in his palm and bringing his thumb arcing downwards across its curve. His melon dropped earthwards, thumping down on Poppy's open sandals. It landed across her toenails, which she'd decorated only that morning, and it galvanised her into immediate summary action.

'Oh!' Poppy squeaked. 'I say, how dare you!'

She took a pace back and whipped her free hand sharply across his cheek-bone. Before this had time to register on the Chief's dazed face, Poppy's melon had come screaming in, slapping viciously against his left temple. He was a solid, imposing man but he rocked nevertheless.

'Now let that be a lesson to you,' Poppy scolded. 'You might get away behaving like that with some people but I won't stand for it.'

She turned and made for the gate as a tear trickled across his numbed cheek.

'Fancy. You a policeman, and all. You should be putting a stop to this sort of thing.'

Poppy swung round, unhindered, and marched out

into the flickering maze beyond.

The dusty road to Damascus, enlivened only by periodic checkpoints, allowed Tommy time to wonder. He and Poppy hadn't seen Jog for six weeks now although parcels at Istanbul had kept them in touch. The Reds had made their usual early surge and were well ahead of a jaded Liverpool. Tommy missed his dad, missed just having him around. He was past the cuddly stage now, though he didn't mind the odd manly arm thrown about his shoulders. Poppy probably missed him more, though she would never admit it.

'Just think. He's lying there, he's got the whole bed to himself. No fighting over pillows. Marvellous! I bet he can't believe his luck!'

'Do you think he's washing regularly?'

'Your dad! I wouldn't count on it. He used to be grubbier than you are now when I first married him. Took me years to train him.'

'I bet he's lying on the settee right now, watching snooker.'

'With his teevee dinner in the microwave. Wonderful.'

He hadn't, Tommy reflected, watched telly for about a month now, probably the longest period in his life since he could remember. And no computers or video games, not since leaving the autobahns. No mates, no Flegg or Grobbo to kid about with. His whole leisure life had been turned upside down. There was only the football with Marc-Marc to keep him in touch. And did he mind?

'Do you?' queried Poppy solicitously, when Tommy tried to explain things to her.

'I dunno. In some ways I do. It'd be great to go down the Youthie tonight, tell 'em what I've been doing, an' have fish and chips on the way home. United are playing away tomorrow. I bet Dad would have taken me.'

On the other hand, Tommy had begun to live with the

prospect of daily adventure, to feel cheated if a day slipped by without incident. How many exciting things happened to him each month, or each year, in Manchester? If you discount the football, not many. Buying a record or a new pair of jeans or winning the pool tournament all made you feel okay but the buzz didn't last.

Tommy's mum gave him a squeeze as they pulled into the suburbs. Squeezes from Poppy were still cool, so long as his mates weren't around.

'I hope you don't regret coming, sweetheart.'

Tommy clicked into cabaret mode, one of his dad's favourites. 'No,' he intoned mournfully, holding a cordless mike at a slight angle from his restless lips. 'No regrets.' Both of them thought of Jog as he did this but it wasn't necessary to mention it. He was on both their minds.

Camping Damas was the focal point for all the overland trips heading south and east. It boasted hot showers and cold beer. Last Exit's pan-African expedition would be holed up there, Haggis informed them, as would the German outfit, Coffin Tours.

They swung off the highway in the late afternoon, somewhere in the northern suburbs. A dusty white wall, maybe a metre high, encircled the sprawling grove of Camping Damas. Last Exit were the first arrivals. The company tipped out, scratching around for a rock-free space on which to erect the tents. Since Blondie was still engaging in some form of entanglement each night with Nokkers, Tommy was continuing to sleep alone. This meant having to erect a tent by himself, usually on a leftover patch of scrub. Employing a handy rock as a mallet, Tommy smirked as he smacked his best skewers into the sandy crust.

Blondie's absence had allowed him to sidestep any

62

unpleasant encounters with a flannel for several days. However, complications with his plumbing had worsened if anything and, two minutes after his handiwork with the tentpegs, Tommy was to be seen haring over to the hanging door of the solitary toilet cubicle.

Hardly had he unbuttoned before engine roar disturbed the relative peace of the site. A second expedition had hit town. The sound of pounding feet heading for the latrines caused a flicker of alarm. Tommy began to whistle loudly and unmelodically. He didn't want to be caught with his pants down.

But it was the showers they were after, next door to the gloomy pit over which Tommy was now concentrating, and a queue had quickly formed.

'Heather, I'm going second in the shower. I know she said on the truck she was second but I'm here so I'll be second. Now, just keep my place, will you, while I go back for my scrubbing brush and just remember that I'm second, even though I'm not here.'

It did not sound too encouraging. They didn't appear to be made of the mettle required for five-a-side. Adjusting his angle of despatch slightly, Tommy listened in dismay as the shrill, complaining voices of the latrine queue joined in.

'Heather, I just hope this toilet is a proper British one. I can't stand these ghastly Asian loos where one is forced to squat. Last time, I got my flip-flops all squelchy.'

Heather couldn't agree more. 'Actually, Claire, I haven't been properly since Amman. Without those lags on the wall, I simply can't get a grip.'

Pungent, lavatorial odours clung to the encampment and by common consent the adventurers set off the next morning, leaving the prissy English girls to slop around in the dark confines of the privy with their prized pink shreds of bogroll.

Three days later, they were in Jerash, a town of spectacular beauty just inside the Jordanian border. The Romans had regarded it as 'fun city', a favourite resort for first century R 'n' R. Jog had bought Tommy a 35mm camera, second hand, as a leaving present and he was now busying himself with the problems of speeds and apertures. Three months ago, he'd have had a job to use a point-and-shoot from the back of a cornflake packet. It was possible, Tommy thought, as he prowled about the perimeter of the theatre, to catch the stage against a background of hills that ringed the city like camel humps.

So absorbed was he that he almost failed to clock the presence of the only two Arab tourists in Jerash. A slight metallic clinking to his rear forewarned him and he swung round.

'How's it going, buddy?' The man was probably in his early forties. He sported a superbly-cut beige suit and a twenty two carat smile. His companion, a Bedouin girl, shaded herself demurely behind her master, her necklaces rustling in the slight breeze like Chinese chimes.

Omar was disappointed to discover Tommy was not from Yoo Ess. He'd schooled there, twelve years at Cincinnati and Kentucky. What was he doing now? Well, on honeymoon.

'No,' Tommy corrected, 'where do you work?'

'Oh, Saudi, man. I sell a few pipes.'

On request, Tommy squinted into Omar's viewfinder and focused on the happy couple, catching the girl's heavily-bejewelled hand as it brushed away a few renegade strands of her burnished cheeks.

'Business going well?'

Omar permitted Tommy another glimpse of his white-and-yellow smile. It was a dazzling advertisement for desert dentistry.

'Aw . . .' he drawled with that sense of understatement

reserved for the very, very rich. 'I make enough to get by.'

Poppy had her sketchbook out by the time Tommy rejoined her. He watched her filling in the details of the forum, but his mind was on other things. He was thirteen but people were treating him like an adult. They spoke to him on adult terms. Back home, they treated him like a kid. Back home, he never really had a conversation with an adult that lasted more than a few seconds.

'Tommy, come down and get your hands washed. Tea's ready.'

'Slip to the offie, there's a good kid, and get us a couple of cans.'

'I can't, Dad. They won't serve me.'

'I'll write you a note.'

'Right. So what was the name given to the Jewish New Year? Tommy?'

'Play on their centre backs, kid. Just run at 'em.'

'Tommy! Time for bed.'

The group travelled down to Amman and beyond to the King's Highway, stopping off for the obligatory bathe in the Dead Sea. Haggis questioned his charges solicitously. 'No cuts or scratches, now?' he enquired. 'They'll only fester.' The adventurers scoured themselves for scabrous surfaces. 'How about you, Blondie?' Haggis probed, fingering his ginger eyebrows in concern.

'Don't worry, mate.' Blondie summoned a weak smile. 'All my scars are emotional. In here.' He tapped his chest lightly and shuffled off to join the others. Nokkers smiled thinly at this, leaving Tommy perplexed. All he knew was that Blondie was back to sleeping in the tent and that regular washes were now back on the agenda.

'Poppy, did you know it's Pinny's birthday tomorrow?' Nokkers had approached, tissue in hand, and she allowed a second or two for Poppy to dislodge the Tarzan rope swaying out of her left nostril before continuing. 'And what with you being a teacher, educated an' all, we wondered if you could knock off a comic verse to go in the card.'

'What a lovely thought. What a lovely, lovely thought.' Tommy had crept up behind his mum and his mimicry captured her exactly.

'Beat it, kid,' growled Nokkers, reaching for a handful of gravel.

Pinny had been travelling for six years and in a few hours she would be thirty. Since her skirmish with the clean-up woman down the autobahn, she had regularly buzzed for a loo stop six or seven times a day. Unless, of course, there was no cover. Crossing the featureless landscapes of Syria and Jordan, Pinny had managed to suppress her urges until the protective cloak of dusk fell.

Poppy delivered her birthday verse at breakfast to universal acclaim. She drew the attention of the company, clapping and clucking, and then wrapped a matronly arm about Pinny's shoulders.

> Please accept this bag of olives with your morning
>   meal
> There are eight of us here who know just how you feel.
> We appreciate your deepest fears
> At reaching that milestone, thirty years.
> But take it from us, it's not as bad as it seems
> Getting accustomed to dentures and facial creams.
> True, rheumatics can be a bit of a bind
> And flatulence leads to friends being unkind.
> But there's whist drives and barn dances and walks in
>   the hills
> You can be almost active if you take the right pills!
> May your health and your wealth in the future stay fine
> And take comfort in this – you only look twenty-nine.

Whoops of harsh antipodean laughter rent the air. Even the English smiled and clapped politely. Tommy burned, mostly with pride but with a flicker of curiosity. He hadn't seen Poppy in the limelight like that before. She didn't act like that at home. She kept herself busy, making the tea and doing the hoovering and whatnot. When she and Jog had friends round, the men did most of the talking, the joking and the waving of the arms. She would just laugh and listen and put the pot on for another coffee. Why? Why, when she could entertain like that did she choose to stay in the shadows? Before they'd set off in the taxi, leaving Jog sprawling all over the bedsheets, Tommy would have said he'd known everything there was to know about his mum.

Later that day, Tommy met Mahad Abu Kasim. The truck turned off the highway for a lunchstop, only to nose into a Bedouin encampment. Mahad, in his forty third year, was monarch of the flapping canvases, uncountable black goats, several litters of children and a superbly maintained NATO issue sub-machine gun. Mahad, hotheaded at seventeen, had shot his brother during a lull in a wedding feast. The state had sentenced him to nine years' imprisonment and the family had tagged on a banishment for a further fifteen. Mahad, however, had prospered. His time of exile was complete. He could, if he wished, partake of a symbolic cup of coffee with his family and return to the fold. Looking up into the clear skies, at the tattered bodies of suspended hawks, keen-eyed warriors of their barren but pylon-free pastures, Mahad confessed that he had a dilemma. Thoughtfully sipping black tea, he explained that his blood pulled him back to the town but that the countryside tugged his sleeve in other directions. Before the adventurers left, Mahad took Tommy to one side and pressed three silver coins in his hand. 'For you,' he whispered. 'From the

Romans.'

'The death-cult city of Petra,' Werner read, 'is also known as The Rock. This tribal stronghold raises mechanical questions as intriguing as the Pyramids.'

Unfortunately for Tommy, mechanical questions were also being raised about the state of his plumbing and as the adventurers left the Bedford to wind their way through the *siq*, the narrow channel that led to the city's heart, Tommy wilted by the wayside. When he defecated now, it came out like a dash of lemonade. Toilet cubicles were irrelevant now, as was toilet tissue. When you were gripped, you were gripped. You dropped your shorts and you did it by the roadside. Stomach cramps had become an unstoppable force in Tommy's life. Pride, dignity. They didn't count. He didn't mind who saw him squatting. Get rid of the cramps, even if only for a few moments, that was the main thing, the only thing.

Poppy was no help, for she had it too. As did Nokkers, Marc-Marc and over half the crew. Since Syria. They'd all been scythed down, almost overnight. The road to Petra was strewn with squatting scarecrows with one hand scrabbling at the rockside for support and the other squeezing the button of a Nikon. 'Me no Leica,' Tommy thought, a brief borrowed flash of humour to lighten a grim scenario.

Blondie, however, was not amongst the sickies. His task on the duty rota had remained unchanged. As the group's only doctor, he had been charged with the daily chlorination of the truck's water tank. For a month, he'd dutifully popped the tabs in each evening until, that is, he read an interesting article in his journal about placebos. Blondie stopped sterilising the water on the day they crossed into Syria. He didn't tell anyone, of course, but he made a note of it in his medical diary. Which is where Tommy found it one evening during a little private research into whether bats might carry rabies. The doctor's diary was closed and carefully replaced. Tommy's thoughts drifted to the six-pack of Perrier water Blondie had been keeping topped up in his locker recently. 'You bastard!' Tommy burst out, airing his venom at Blondie's side of the tent. He pulled his gear out, too angry to cry, and set off in search of Poppy.

Cap was at his most loquacious on the long slog back to the Turkish border. He began after an innocent remark from Werner about camels. 'Yair. Didja know Australia actually exports camels to the Middle East? We're the world's biggest exporter of camels.' The Arabian strain, he informed all those within earshot, which meant everybody, had become weakened and disease-ridden. In contrast, those exported to Australia during the last century had gone forth and multiplied. In the 1980s, the trade had been reversed.

'I wouldn't have believed it!' burst out an astonished Poppy. 'That's a wonderful story.'

'Oh, there's a lot of things you don't know about Australia,' continued Cap, warming to his task. 'Didja know it gets more snow per annum than Switzerland?' Even the sickies writhing from Blondie's experiment stilled themselves at this revelation. 'And,' stressed Cap, pausing dramatically before the delivery of his third blockbuster, 'Australia is the biggest exporter of rice in the world.'

It was a long haul back through Syria and little was spoken. Poppy had had one of her quiet words with Cap, being a countryman of Blondie's, as to the reasons for Tommy's withdrawal from his tent. Cap had nodded thoughtfully, strapped on his Bowie knife, and then turned in cold anger with his jaw set.

He caught Blondie on all fours, beating bugs off his sleeping sheet in the late afternoon sun.

'I think you've got a job to do that needs doing, John.'

Blondie glanced up, curious at both the tone in Cap's voice and at his choice of appellation.

'Oh, yeah. What's that?'

The Australian went down on his haunches so as to meet Blondie at eye-level.

'Right now. Before anyone else gets ill.'

He delved into the back pocket of his shorts and produced a sheet, folded meticulously into quarters.

'Go on. Open it up. Open it up and read it.'

'What's the matter, Cap? Sun too hot for yer?' Blondie flicked the paper apart with his thumbnail and glanced down to read.

DANGEROUS
UNFIT TO DRINK

Like most very fair people, Blondie avoided too much sun and, even after a few years' doctoring in Alice, his friends would still describe him as pale. By the time he looked up from Cap's note, he had gone the colour of bone, bleached by the desert sun.

'You know what I'm talking about, don't you?'

Blondie nodded.

'Jenny's been crook all week, Alison's off her food and that poor kid Tommy's been holding his guts for a fortnight.'

Blondie knew that if he opened his mouth in defence, he'd have been decked. For there was none. You don't experiment with the health of unsuspecting kids on holiday. He kept his lips tight and his eyes on the sleeping sheet.

'So I'll tell yer what yer goin' to do, John. After you put the notice up, you're goin' to make an announcement. You're goin' to get everybody together and then you'll

70

explain yerself and make a public apology. Do I make myself clear?'

'Yair.' Blondie had barely opened his lips to reply and if Cap hadn't been kneeling on the same sheet, he wouldn't have heard. Cap picked a dead bug off the corner of the fabric, tossed it to one side and strolled away.

'You stupid bar-stard!' Nokkers hissed, as the assembly listened to Blondie's monotone delivery. Blondie himself stood by the truck, his arm resting on it for support.

'That was a bloody silly thing to do, John,' Haggis added, using, like Cap, his first name as a reprimand. 'I think you owe us all a beer.'

'Whooo! Great! Does that go for me as well?' Tommy leapt from the rock that had served as his stool. Under normal circumstances, there would have been laughs and slaps on the back at his spontaneity but on this occasion there was only silence.

6

ON THE PERSIAN CARPET

Everyone approached Iran with trepidation, even though the revolution had taken place when Tommy was marauding around the floor in nappies. They made the crossing at the scruffy border town of Dogubayazit, lying in the shadow of Mount Ararat. X-ray photographs had recently detected a large, boat-shaped structure moulded into the mountain and Old Nick, the theology student, was putting forward a case for it being Noah's Ark.

The debate took their minds off politics for a while. At least until they hit the line of wagons curling all the way around the base of Ararat and tailing well back into Turkey. Haggis clocked the queue at a modest twenty five kilometres. Tommy counted 3000 trucks awaiting entry. Some of the European drivers had been there three days.

There was nothing heading westwards so Haggis pulled out and crawled past them. The girls all waved at the truckers like whores on a holiday. Nokkers blew kisses to several neanderthals lumped about the tarmac and was rewarded by a series of curious gestures with the arm and elbow. No-one appeared to object to the blatant queue-jumping. Within half a day, they were through to the administration block.

Waiting in line, Tommy glanced at some of the posters slapped invitingly about. One faded relic illustrated a bushy-browed ayatollah curling his lip over the daunting caption:

OUR AIM IS THE TOTAL DESTRUCTION OF THE SUPER-POWERS

A second displayed a promiscuous Statue of Liberty. A manacled, horribly mutilated body lay impaled upon its lipsticked spikes, blood gushing over the statue's robes. It was entitled 'Democracy'.

'I think I prefer "Skegness is so bracing", don't you?' Poppy remarked to a knot of baffled Aussies.

The group began to reassemble at the truck some three quarters of an hour later. After a hesitant roll over two gigantic flags on the tarmac, intended to humiliate drivers of the USA and the Soviet Union, the truck was on its way, heading for Tabriz, Tehran and Esfahan. It was the trade route to Pakistan. Haggis didn't intend putting any frills on this leg of the journey. It was to be a straight six-day slog with the hammer down. Mostly, there were patches of vegetation lying on either side of the highway but beyond that, the hills were brown and barren. Between the towns, ramshackle buildings of mud and plaster housed the peasantry. Tommy was intrigued to see how many had bent TV aerials protruding from the rooftops.

About this time, the gifts of fruit began. There was little local traffic on the road but what there was tooted and pipped in acknowledgement. A grey saloon overtook in a long, lazy manoeuvre. Its side window was wound down and an apple tossed onto the truck. Then another. The passenger had a basketful on the back seat. The adventurers cheered and hooted. A shower of produce followed, twenty apples tossed in with pinpoint precision. Amid wild applause, the saloon pulled back and drifted

73

into the dusty haze. Two motorcyclists materialised. As they cut out to overtake, the pillion passenger lobbed a sack of cucumbers into the gangway. The machine wobbled alarmingly, then sped on into a dustcloud. The grey saloon reappeared, its back seat stocked with tempting ammunition: dates, melons, olives and a replenished supply of eating apples.

A portable feast ensued. Conversation flowed on famous binges and binge-ers. Alison stole the limelight with her favourite tale about Luigi, the fat boy from Koonoomoo.

'There's this fat kid, Luigi. I mean, really fat. He waddles into school with this enormous tucker-box full of spaghetti sarnies. All the kids waddle along behind him going, "Hey, Luigi!"'

Alison's expert mimicry was interrupted by a shocked whisper from her mother. Jenny had caught sight of a solemn Herr Bolsterley sitting further down the truck. Having politely declined all offers of fruit on account of his 'condition', Werner had set about a light lunch of charcoal. The unpredictable bumping of the truck had led to substantially more of the black stuff being smeared about his face than had been popped down his bolt-hole. This rather alarming vision was framed by Werner's thick, grizzly, grey beard.

'Look at him,' Jenny hissed in wonder. 'He's eating charcoal.'

'Jees!' gasped Alison, dropping out of her Mediterranean posturing in astonishment. 'He looks like an Abo!'

Later, at a chai stop, Poppy and Tommy fell into conversation with a medical assistant who claimed to have returned a fortnight earlier from Iowa. Inevitably, the subject turned to politics.

'What is your impression of Iran?'

Poppy searched for the diplomatic reply. She spoke of

the gifts of the Iranian people and counterbalanced that with criticism of the high prices and administrative chaos.

'Yes, you are right!' The assistant leapt in swiftly. 'But this is the necessary dust of the revolution. My people must make sacrifices until we become self-sufficient. And my people will make those sacrifices!' His eyes blazed, challenging Poppy or Tommy to counter.

Two days further on, outside Yazd, the tricky topic of western opinion cropped up again. Barely before the first adobe rooftops of the town had been sighted, the truck ran into a gauntlet of checkpoints manned by provincial hooligans. Some were militia, some wore hand-me-downs from the revolution and others were regular soldiers. It was the army who boarded the truck, granite-faced and hell-bent on intimidation. Four soldiers spaced themselves along the gangway, automatic rifles at the ready. The adventurers cowered. An officer heaved himself aboard, promenaded the length of the aisle and then paused to twizzle his swagger-stick. His eyes raked the company, locking eventually into those of a seriously scared Dormouse. Dormouse, a Scots girl, was the least loquacious of the whole band. She spent at least ninety per cent of her time aboard the truck asleep and most of the rest yawning. The officer had caught her in one of her rare waking moments.

'Tell me,' he leered, taking an obvious delight in Dormouse's discomfiture. 'What is your opinion of Iran?'

Their fate seemed to hinge on a diplomatic response. Dormouse's eyes rolled vacantly about her head. Cap attempted to intercede.

'We've all been very impressed by . . .'

The officer's voice cut through the air. 'Not you, mister. I am asking this one.' He stuck his cane belligerently at Dormouse.

'I . . . I . . . that is, we all think it's a good p-place a-and

75

the p-people are very friendly.'

'No!' The officer's cane thrashed across the metal roof support behind Dormouse's head. 'You are wrong!' He threw his head back and brayed with laughter. 'Iran is a bad place and it is full of bad people.' The soldiers, mystified by this sudden change of atmosphere, threw their heads back and brayed likewise. The adventurers shrank into their seats. Gaily, the officer skipped back along the aisle, followed by his shuffling minions. 'Enjoy your stay!' he bawled. 'Have a nice time in Iran.'

Zahedan, their next supply point, lay on the far side of the Great Sand Desert, close to the Pakistani border. Temperatures had climbed into the hundreds. Vast, coloured dunes drifted by, fifty metres tall. Lofty metal rods were positioned at intervals along the tarmac for those periodic occasions when sand obliterated the highway. The town itself, when they arrived, appeared a cosmopolitan kitchen of thieves. It was as if the riff-raff of the Orient had scuffed their way there and got no further. Punishing deserts lay on all sides. Indians, Pakistanis, Chinese, Afghans, Iranians and Nepalese congregated there, pushing mischievously against the adventurers as they foraged for provisions.

Intact, barely, the party pushed on into the dark, throwing up a camp against a railway line. An ancient railway attendant with white, flowing hair and a swinging hurricane lamp tottered up to bid welcome and recite Kipling.

At three in the morning, Pinny woke up screaming. A scorpion had negotiated her sewn-in groundsheet and embarked on an ambitious tour of her armpit. Volunteers to extricate it were few. Blondie, finally, won back a little esteem as he slipped sweatily into her writhing canvas armed with a pair of tweezers. It was a difficult man-oeuvre in the dark, compounded by Pinny's roars and the huge, tufty banks of hair beneath her armpit, into which the scorpion was now happily entangled. By the time Blondie emerged with his out-nipped adversary, leaving an exhausted Pinny beneath the limp flaps, the rank smell of fear clung to them all and it remained with them until first light.

But by then, the Pakistani border was in view.

7

PUNCTURED IN PAKISTAN

The signs were not encouraging for travellers in Pakistan. The graded border road, from Taftan to Quetta, enveloped the sickies in the back in a thick, choking cloud of dust. Haggis pulled over onto the desert tracks and things improved marginally.

A hundred kilometres short of Quetta, they came across Last Exit's sister vehicle on the Asian run, a museum piece held together by gum and goodwill. It was six weeks out of Kathmandu. Like Eskimos, the trucks rubbed noses in greeting and the travellers spilled out for the exchange of news.

There had been several serious attempts to loot the homegoing truck as it had bulldozed its way through Pakistan's Sind province and boarders had had to be repelled in a series of fistfights. The truck had stalled outside a local school on the bell. Three hundred cheering kids had stormed out for an improvised game of cricket. They opted to bowl first, using rocks in the absence of balls and the truck as a slightly oversized wicket. The visitors' only run was the one the driver made for the cab. An American passenger, finally, had been relieved of $1000 in Lahore, despite strapping her money belt firmly to her person before turning in for the night. Haggis listened to all this in silence, nodding his head sagely from time to time. Looking round at the drawn faces of his tiny band, he meditated for some moments before delivering a reply. 'Sounds a bit too quiet for my liking.'

The acrid smell of tear-gas greeted the adventurers at Quetta. They'd missed a riot by thirty minutes. Armed police were lined the length of Jinnah Road, decked out like samurai and grinning sheepishly. Tommy bought a paper. Bands of bloodthirsty dacoits were on the rampage, looting and burning at will. One plucky village had formed a vigilante group and a ferocious battle had ensued when the dacoits fell against it. Four robbers had been slain, including their leader, the notorious Basho the Bandit.

It wasn't necessary to take a vote about moving on. Haggis forked out for a hotel and they were out of it at first light, across the Bolan Pass and on to Jhatpat. It wasn't a wise move.

The area had been a centre for riot and demonstration for weeks. Body counts were a daily occurrence. Jhatpat was on a short fuse when Haggis decided to stop for a Coke, at that time of day when even the broad details of people's faces are being lost to shadow.

In seconds, the truck was besieged by a jostling, unpleasant throng of several hundred men. After a short, terse discussion, the adventurers decided to see it through and grab a Coke. Ten minutes. Tommy had barely had time to complain about the shards of glass swimming about his foaming brew before the warning came. An official placed his hand upon Poppy's shoulder and breathed hotly into her ear. 'There is no safety for you here. Go now.' Quickly butting their way back to the truck, he and Poppy caught the attention of some of the stragglers. They too were leaving, their splintered drinks unfinished.

It took the full force of Cap's barrack-room roar to

dislodge the press about the truck's rear entrance. They slackened momentarily and he was able to gouge his way through, followed by Alison then Jenny. The girls following behind emerged less unscathed. The mood of the crowd had changed from the mischievous to the malevolent. It had begun to clap and chant and jeer with hideous intent. The more public-spirited stood on its edges, whistling with shrill urgency at Haggis and willing him to take flight.

At this point, Sally opened the cab in a vain effort to check numbers. Haggis was revving furiously, ready for instant departure. Sally's move was the catalyst the mob had been seeking. Surging forward, a dozen brown hands pulled her down as a crush of bodies scrambled into her seat, thrusting for the ignition key. The prissy English girls began to shriek. Nokkers grabbed a beer bottle.

The police came from nowhere, a line of five or six uniformed heroes wielding lathees. They cut into the crowd without quarter, lashing the backs of the less wary with their swishing weaponry and delivering resounding slaps to the faces of the more fortunate. In seconds, Sally had been deposited in the cab and Haggis was away.

The adventurers effected their successful escape for about a kilometre, leaving behind the swaying lamps and tumult of the town for the pitch of the countryside. As Dormouse, in a rare wakeful moment, harangued all those within earshot about the high incidence of ambush and pillage locally, disaster struck. A hellish crash sent the truck slewing to a halt. Tommy's first assumption was that a tree had been felled across the road. For a second, all was still and then bodies, naked writhing bodies, began slithering from the ditches and disentangling themselves from the undergrowth. Back in the town, where there was light, a rippling wave of rioters flooded the highway, out of the jurisdiction of the men with lathees and kicking out for the truck with fiendish intent.

Haggis was out of his cab in seconds. 'It's the bloody water tank. It's sheared off!' The brown, metal tank lay thirty metres back. The wild men from the ditches watched with polite interest. The mob was hurtling on, almost out of the lights now and into the darkness. Haggis precipitated a response. 'It'll mean two days without water.'

Cap's voice rose up a heartbeat later, with the raw courage of an NCO exhorting his men over the trenches. 'Okay, lads, let's go for it!'

With the exception of Werner, who had been confined to Sickies' Quarters since his charcoal-eating exploits, every other male plus Nokkers leaped over the side. The tank, half-filled with water, weighed like concrete. The whoops of the mischief-makers had ceased to become distinct and were now deafening. Six men jockeyed round the container. A dozen sweaty palms fought for position and leverage.

'Now!' Cap barked. With the precision of soldiers presenting arms, knees and elbows jerked upright. The tank rose to calf height.

'Move!' It was Cap again, exhorting them on. The hot breath of the mob was almost at their necks. No-one dared turn for fear of losing impetus but the screams of the English girls, like anguished punters at the finishing-line, told Tommy that it might well be a photo finish. Lurching and staggering, they covered first twenty metres, then thirty. The howling pack was within rock-throwing distance. A half-brick clattered against one of the metal roof supports, ricocheting off into the night. They were there. The rear door swung open.

'Up!'

One gigantic groan rent the darkness. The tank

teetered teasingly a hand's span below the gangway and then fell back.

'Again!'

Something struck Tommy on the back of his head. Something relatively soft, like a potato. For the first time in his life, he saw stars blazing across the heavens without having to look up at the sky. But the tip of the tank had landed in the aisle. They didn't need to be told to shove. Blondie, then Nokkers were both hit by missiles. At this range, they could hardly be missed.

'Hang on!' The adventurers dived for the sides, reaching for the roof supports. Big Nick had flung himself halfway across the gangway, his legs trailing in the dust as the truck began to move off. He was bleeding at the forehead. Cap was the last to launch himself at the vehicle. He rubbed a hand through the shaken Nick's hair as Haggis picked up speed. Missiles were already falling short of them. 'She'll be right, mate,' the Australian said, in a remarkably even tone.

Haggis didn't stop until Sukkur was behind them. Traffic had become heavier and every truck had its quota of armed guards, squatting watchfully from above the load into the gloom. Finding a camp site proved difficult. Several times Haggis pulled over between villages at a likely spot, only to find it submerged by water. The last strike of the monsoon had only been a week previous. Finally, at a slightly higher elevation, they hit upon a flat, drained area. It was difficult in the gloom to ascertain how big a site they had stumbled across but it seemed comparable to a cricket pitch. There were no lights in evidence, save for the convoys thundering by some thirty metres away, and not a sound to indicate human habitation. Cautiously, the adventurers began to disembark.

Within two minutes, a good-humoured crowd of

maybe a hundred had assembled, mostly around the cooking area. Books had slipped away before their arrival to resume hostilities with her blocked bowels. Of all the company, she alone had had the audacity to suffer from constipation.

Jenny, meanwhile, had seated herself on a camp stool and was quizzing a throng of eager Pakistanis about Australia's glorious cricketing past. They could rarely be faulted, answering easily and with confidence. One shiny-eyed boy, a spindly soul in wretched garb, stood out above the others. Jenny warmed to his alertness.

'I know you probably have to go to school here.' She indicated the surrounding gloom with a wave. 'But later, would you like to come to live in Australia?'

The boy's answer expressed genuine puzzlement. 'Why?' He gazed round at the adventurers' belongings as they were being transported to their crescent of canvas, possessions he could never hope to attain, and then at his own ragged family. 'I am very happy here. I love my country. Why should I wish to move?'

Books came thudding back, breaking into the circle, consumed with horror. 'I say, you lot! Guess what? I've just had my first public crap.' A tiny band of locals had become attracted by her wheezes of concentration as she squatted in the darkness. They had remained undetected until she turned her head in a moment of copric despair. Four concerned men hovered behind her, agonising at her distress. 'Push, missy, push!' their leader had urged. Whatever had been forthcoming from her pasty, sullen buttocks shrank back, like a snail into its shell. Books had lifted up her skirts and fled, leaving a few hopeful sheets of loo roll for the puzzled quartet to ponder over. Back at the truck, even by the faint light of the lanterns, Books' face spoke volumes.

It took a further eighteen hours to reach Lahore. The

83

outskirts of the city resembled an open wound as piles of tortured flesh lay slumped across the roadside in various stages of decay. Bodies lay heaped on blackened piles of refuse or sprawled across canvas mattresses. Lanterns swung vigorously from shop doorways as vendors and the public stepped over the corpses of the homeless to transact their business. The more sensitive of the company drew fingers across their eyes as if at a horror show, keeping them displayed there until Haggis turned in to The Mall, a well-appointed heirloom from the Raj. Traffic was relatively light and in no time the Bedford had crunched to a halt on the gravel of the Intercontinental Hotel.

By nine, having breakfasted, Tommy set out with a full itinerary planned. Since the hotel was a couple of kilometres or so up the unfashionable end of The Mall, Tommy decided on a brisk walk to the city's more central attractions. The local force of rickshaw-wallahs thought otherwise. They dogged him relentlessly, hurling reassurance and bargain basement prices at his every other pace.

'You come with me, mister. I am good Pakistani. Not agit-man.'

'Only four rupees, mister. Only three rupees.'

Poppy, who had decided to give the day over to a little pampering, courtesy of the hotel masseur, seemed a long way off as Tommy strode into the Post Office, inky letters to Flegg and Grobbo in his sticky palms. After collecting the mail from the poste restante counter, Tommy had been given carte blanche. He had $150 in his belt and the day to himself.

Devastating strikes had led to United mounting their best campaign in years. The roars of the crowd could be heard across the city at Maine Road and they'd signed a lad from a small Southern Irish side who, Jog thought, had the makings of another George Best. Tommy looked up rapturously from his bench outside the post office into the spinning brown eyes of a highly-excited Pakistani who, like himself, seemed delirious with joy. Mr Mujahid Saleem, employee of the Government Department of Finance, glanced at Tommy's letters still for despatch and blinked with happiness.

'My esteemed and cherished sir, do I understand from your magnetic and attractive epistles that you are an Englishman?'

Tommy nodded slightly at the podgy, heaving figure before him.

'Sir, you have set my fastidious heart dancing with joy. I am ecstatic and jubilant. I am raptic. I am rejoicing to the core of my heart.'

As Tommy surveyed the eager, fat face before him, his wariness evaporated. A thick, friendly moustache sagged doggily below his upper lip. Dark sunglasses failed to conceal the soft, spaniel-like eyes behind. This comic vision was made complete by a thick and juicy cowlick, slithering like a pendulum across the clerk's oily forehead.

Mujahid leaned forward conspiratorially. 'The Omniscient, sir, has gifted me with swift and brisk speaking powers which might create thrills and spills during your sojourn in Lahore. As one who is not only working in some lowly government office on a meagre salary but who is also studying in the evening classes (Post-graduate in English Literature), I am obliged to enquire whether you might contemplate passing the day in my company making chitterings, tittle-tattle and gossip?'

Half-heartedly, Tommy began to protest. 'It's very kind of you to offer but I leave your beautiful city tomorrow. Today it is necessary for me to . . .'

Mujahid was already steering him out of the building and into an adjacent coffee-house. 'There is always time.

Tell me, sir, do you not believe, in company with Ruskin, that the boredom of travelling is in exact proportion to the speed in which it is done?'

Nokkers rescued him seven hours later. Mujahid had been explaining to Tommy, with the help of the local matrimonial columns, the difficulties of finding a bride.

'My son, Muslim (Sunni), 27, tall, handsome electronics engineering graduate, monthly salary 30,000 rupees. Proposals invited from educated families permanently settled in U.S.A. The girl be 20, beautiful, educated, slim, height 5' 4". Box No . . .'

'Beautiful, charming, graceful, tall, slim, 24, B.Sc.Hons., daughter of Upian Sunni high Govt. officer living in posh locality desires matrimonial with C.E., B.E., M.B.B.S., M.B.A. or Class 1 officer of equally respectable family. Boy should be in early thirties . . .'

'So you perceive, my esteemed and honoured companion, the insurmountable difficulties faced by a humble minion and lackey such as myself.'

They were approaching the Zam Zam gun now, a monstrous fixed barrel made famous by Kipling. Its highly polished brass gleamed in the sun and Nokkers sat astride it, idly stroking its hot, burnished length.

'I wish only that my fiancé should be untouched by concupiscence, salaciousness or lasciverousness.'

A cloud passed across Tommy's already numbed face.

'Tommy, I wish my girl to be a virgin.'

Nokkers, swinging her legs easily across the barrel, summed up the situation in a flash. Her green vest lifted in the slight breeze caused as she sprang to the ground and headlocked Mujahid in her downy grip.

'Well there ain't no virgins round here, pal. Didn't he tell ya, he's travellin' with Australians.'

She released Mujahid's shocked head from the

choking confines of her bosom and took a pace back, leering. His swift and brisk speaking powers had deserted him, perhaps for the first time in his life. Mujahid fled, doomed to impecunious and inconsolable bachelorhood and celibacy. Tommy stood there, dazed and swaying, his domestic news from Manchester as yet unread.

Back at the hotel, the air was full of expectancy. Virtually every single girl in the party was assembled on the lawns, in a skittish sort of queue. Pinny, Sally, Miss Swiss and Alison, they were all there. Even Dormouse had pulled herself off her sleeping sheet for a brief salute to the sun.

The cause of the excitement was the hotel masseur, a handsome, well-framed Pakistani in his late thirties. His starched whites were creased impeccably, offset by a natty bowtie which added to his general air of distinction. A fee of fifty rupees had been agreed on shortly after Tommy's departure to the post office and already he had had a string of satisfied clients, many of whom were turning up for seconds. Nokkers, with her intuitive feel for a good time, pushed effortlessly to the front of the queue.

Whatever it was he was doing, armed with his strong hands and aromatic oils, he was doing it within the secret confines of the canvas. Perhaps he had trade secrets he wished not to give way. The average length of a massage seemed to be running at about forty minutes though, curiously, it wouldn't have been unfair to say that the prettier you were the longer it took.

The men had all drifted away, browsing over newspapers or sipping at coffee in the hotel lounge. The Rugby World Cup was in progress and the Aussie contingent were following with interest. They had made it to the semis and Cap reckoned that in Campese they had the match winner. Only Big Nick hung about the tents, watching Alison giggling with the others and feeling a faint, unusual pang of jealousy.

To Tommy's horror, the tent currently attracting attention was the one his mum shared with Pinny. And as Pinny was standing in full view, clasping her raw little hands together and jumping up and down, there could be little doubt as to who was currently on the receiving end of the masseur's nimble fingers. 'Oooh! That's lovely. Lovely!'

'Go for it, Poppy!' Nokkers yelled earthily, between swigs at the bottle neck of a local brew.

'Hill,' Pinny confided, as she reached out for a proffered slug. 'He minipulated areas I niver knew ixisted.'

'Ooooh! Oooh!' Poppy's moans were longer now and unabated. Tommy fidgeted. He felt torn between slobbing down with his Reds' programmes in the hotel lounge and staying to protect his mum, if it was protection she needed. In Jog's absence, he was the man of the household. If his mum was in trouble, he had to be there.

His dilemma was solved, though, by Poppy's unsteady emergence from the tent a moment later, a strange beatific smile upon her face and with eyes that couldn't seem quite to focus. Behind her, the masseur raised himself from his haunches, slapped his palms across each other and grinned wolfishly.

'Ooooh!' Poppy murmured, bewildered by the sudden shafts of sunlight beaming down upon her puckered cheeks. 'I don't know what it is he does, but if you could only bottle it and sell it at Sainsbury's. Ooooh!'

Tommy cocked his head to one side and looked at his mum with a mixture of bafflement and disgust.

'Who's next, ladies?'

'Me! Me!'

It continued until, of all the adults, only Big Nick remained. Was there any point of Sir's anatomy, the

masseur wondered, that might require specialist attention? Big Nick paused, flicking a glance over his shoulder
at where Alison had been standing. But she'd wandered
off, sulking, her fifty rupee note crumpled hotly in her
palm. 'You're not going in there, my girl,' Jenny had
instructed, nodding at the masseur's unzipped theatre of
operation. 'He wouldn't pull any funny stuff with us.
We're women and we can look after ourselves. Just
remember, you're still a girl.'

'Er, well actually,' Nick muttered, breathing into a
perfumed ear, 'I've been getting a bit of discomfort here.'
His hand strayed to the back of his shorts as he patted his
coccyx. 'Too many hot curries, hey.'

To everyone's delight, and to Big Nick's alarm, the
masseur decided that this next demonstration should be a
public one. He commandeered a couple of sleeping mats
from Books' tent and instructed Nick to place himself face
down upon them, naked save for a hand towel placed
over his buttocks and private parts.

This routine quickly drew a crowd. Alison materialised,
clinging to the fringes though Tommy organised himself a
ringside seat. Whatever the elixir was, he wanted to
know. His day-pack, stuffed with riveting statistics from
3000 miles away, dropped to the floor. Jog wouldn't
have believed it.

Pinning Big Nick face down on the mat, the professional settled his own body weight, knees folded, above
the region where Nick's buttocks ended and his legs
began. Exerting himself upwards by a straightening of the
arms, the Pakistani hovered a few inches above Nick's
vulnerable rump. Fractionally, and with admirable control, the masseur allowed his left knee to drop. It rested
momentarily on the fleshy inside of Nick's thighs then
gently nudged down, pressing them apart. His probes left
Nick's legs splayed at an angle of not less than sixty

degrees. Between them, his canopied genitalia hung, loose and unprotected. A thrill of expectation ran through the crowd.

Like a precision parachutist, the Pakistani manoeuvred himself into position. Gradually, he began to descend. His knees, balled tightly together, were the first part of his bulk to make contact with Nick's rolling testicles. The masseur held himself suspended such that this action became nothing more than a slight rubbing. Angling his neck up on one side, Nick caught sight of Jenny, then Sally, then Alison.

Abruptly, the Pakistani released his entire body weight onto Nick's helpless, unsuspecting nuts. He screamed. As they spread out, pinioned to the polymat by ninety kilos of unrelenting muscle, the crowd gasped in horror. They shrank back as one, disturbed at the appalling prospect of discovering two split sacs splattered over the blue polystyrene. And yet, as the Pakistani raised himself aloft, Nick, on the verge of fainting, felt tentatively between his legs and found himself intact. It was as if a man had walked across a floor display of fine, ripe plums and left them unsplit. Bruised, purple but unsplit.

The Pakistani leaped off Big Nick in triumph. Whoops and cheers erupted from the crowd. 'Tell me, sir,' the professional declaimed, milking the applause with obvious relish, 'would it be true to say that your coccygeal pains are now behind you?'

The audience hooted. Big Nick slunk off to the relative safety of his canvas as the Pakistani assumed celebrity status.

'I suppose,' Pinny hypothesised, to no-one in particular and to the world in general, 'we'd be better just to call him Nick from now on.'

'My dear ladies, dinner will not be served for another three quarters of an hour. Perhaps I can be of further assistance?'

Excited giggles greeted his proposal, intermingled with suggestions that 50 rupees was an impossible price for poor western girls to pay. Their carping over finance was greeted with magnanimity.

'So, you pay me what you can. If I can perform a service for you, that is payment enough. Now, who is to be first?'

Despite a chorus of shrill English voices, it was Nokkers who barged forwards, a folded five hundred rupee note clenched between her teeth.

'There's a girl who believes in putting her money where her mouth is,' Jenny observed snidely, once Nokkers was safely out of earshot.

Light was beginning to fade and, even as she approached, a foolhardy mosquito landed on Nokker's arm. Chivalrously, the Pakistani flicked it off as he made his next perfectly reasonable announcement.

'I fear, ladies, that we will be eaten alive if we continue the massage al fresco. Might I suggest that you retire to the privacy of your tents and I will treat each of you in turn.'

Three hours later, after dinner, Tommy overheard Books wittering on to Nokkers about the massage.

'I say, Kate, that Paki bloke, how long did he take with you?'

The English girls alone, of all the nationalities aboard, could not bring themselves to address a member of their own gender in such crude sexist terms, not that Nokkers gave a damn.

'Mmm. An hour and a quarter. So someone told me.'

'Well, how come I only got eight minutes thirty seconds? And another thing, didn't you find he went a bit near the knicker elastic?'

Nokkers sank back into the accommodating arms of

her settee. 'Knickers?' she murmured abstractedly. 'What were you wearing knickers for?'

The adventurers left Lahore with mixed feelings. Tommy was looking forward to Gilgit and the mountains. Others were loth to travel for Lahore Dog had struck them down with a vengeance. The prissy English couple, for example, had totalled nineteen evacuations and four chunders between them since the previous evening. They'd accepted a loaded samosa each from a well-wisher in the bazaar. Along with half a dozen other sickies, they lolled wanly about the front end as the truck crossed the traffic tooting past the Intercontinental and trundled off to the mountains.

The plains were quickly exchanged for tufty, hillocky regions of reddish soil. Haggis drove until eleven, stopping in the centre of a dreary ribbon development village to buy vegetables. Permanent shops of breeze-block construction faced each other at a distance of thirty metres. Spilling between them was a tangle of soft drink stalls and impromptu piles of melons. Through the centre of this clutter ran the road.

Tommy strolled towards one of the less squalid stalls. In the absence of the proprietor, one of the two genial locals lounging about selected a bottle from a lurid green polystyrene cooler and handed it to Tommy.

'I see you are from the United Kingdom, sir.'

Tommy shuddered for a moment, considering the possibility that he had encountered a mystic of extra-ordinary properties who was about to divulge the very moment and nature of Tommy's death. He then noticed the truck's GB plates sparkling in the sunlight and relaxed.

'That's right.' Fiddling with his bottle cap, Tommy inspected the sweet fluid for foreign bodies, specifically glass. 'Have you been there?' It was the sort of question travellers ask politely, knowing full well that most of these idlers merely wished to show off their quaint schoolboy English and would, in all probability, never leave the confines of their breezeblocked gloom.

'I have actually, sir. Seven times. You see, this is not my home. I work for Saudi Airlines and am presently visiting friends.'

Tommy's podgy acquaintance drew another Fanta from the cooler, expertly flicking its top into the dust. 'I liked the United Kingdom very much. Stoke-on-Trent was my favourite place. It will always be very close to my heart.'

Haggis was determined to push on to Islamabad. He knew of a motel on the outskirts of the city, just off the main highway. It was dark by the time he pulled over and raining steadily. There were no other overnighters. The vacant rooms set out in strips looked sad and mournful in the manner of Bates' Motel. Around them, lethargic bushes sprouted, heavy with water. The gloom seemed to embrace the adventurers too, circling round them like a mist until visibility was close to nil. Mostly, they retired early, to catch up with their diaries or to take advantage of an early night.

Alison had stayed awake, though, and Tommy was in the act of brushing past her in his search for a Fanta when she caught his arm. There were rooms to spare and tonight she was on her own.

'Come on in and crash out for a bit,' she urged, pressing Tommy's arm between her thumb and fore-finger. 'I've got plenty of drinks. Save yourself the safari.'

Ensconced on her bed minutes later, Tommy slurped at all the loose liquid careering about the ring-pull and attempted to fill Alison in on the progress of United's season so far.

But he was a naive Red in the presence of a scarlet woman.

'Tomm-my.' Alison drew out the last syllable of his name as she reached for her baby lotion. 'Didn't you ever wonder what went on inside that tent?'

'What tent?' Tommy sprang off her quilt, ensuring that both his feet were touching the floor.

'You know, in Lahore. What do you think that guy was actually doing?' She squirted a generous blob of lotion into her palm. The container was nearly empty and it made a loud farting noise as it blew into her hand. She replaced the bottle and rubbed its creamy contents over both palms, dabbing at a blob that had dropped onto the bare flesh at the end of her shorts. 'C'mon. Lie down.'

Tommy panicked. It wasn't that he didn't want to be there. He did. He didn't know what was coming though he knew he'd probably find it pleasurable But how did you act? What did you do? She knew. She was older. She had all the knowledge and that wasn't fair, especially when boys were supposed to take the lead. Caught between conflicting emotions, not to mention a willy that was growing increasingly restless beneath his trackie bottoms. Tommy decided the only way was out.

'Gotta go now.' He leaped for the door, gripping its handle like an old friend.

'Lie down. Take off your T-shirt.' Alison hadn't moved off the side of the bed. She hadn't stopped fooling around with the cream either but she was staring directly at him now and her eyes were deadly serious.

'See ya tomorrow. Thanks for the drink.' Tommy swung his body clockwise into the dark and bolted.

As he threw himself beneath the sleeping-sheet, his programmes still in his day-pack, still neglected for the most part, growls of laughter broke through from the adjoining chalet. Nokkers and Marc-Marc had hitched up for the night.

'Just like pulling beer from a pump,' he heard Nokkers snicker.

'Yair,' came the reply. 'Two tugs and it comes in buckets.'

Tommy closed his eyes perplexed, wishing he was older.

Two days later, en route to the mountain fastness of Gilgit and its volatile inhabitants, Tommy caught his first sight of the High Karakorams. They were further than they looked. The adventurers travelled on all the next day, a Sunday, and still appeared to get no closer. But the locals provided other compensations. They were the hardy descendants of warrior tribes, solemn, large-framed men with grizzled, ginger beards. The ginger, Werner was quick to explain, was the result of numerous applications of henna; concealment of grey hairs belied their true age.

Beyond Batagram, the road hung precariously above the turquoise waters of the Indus. Periodically, its foundations had crumpled and fallen away, making progress negligible at times. Huge, truck-sized boulders blocked the route at intervals.

It took a further two days' careful negotiation to enter the Gilgit region. It had become much bleaker and more remote. There was only one road now, cut across by numerous military checkpoints. Haggis pulled over at one of them in search of a chai house.

Tommy was the first to find it, a square, smoky room littered with mattresses and low tables. Inside, the candidate for the Northern Areas Council, Mr Shah Jehan, was accounting for the regional strife.

'Here we are too remote from the centres of population. Because of this, they give us no power, no facilities. They take our money in taxes but give us nothing in exchange.' He paused to smile at the bunch of shivering westerners before him. 'And now my people have had enough. That is why there are so many agents of the state in evidence.' He gestured to the army checkpoint outside as the single report of a rifle echoed around the room.

Tommy glanced at the posters and political slogans pinned to the wooden supports and rafters. Prior to this trip, his only interest in politics had been when playing darts in the garage. Jog had a faded poster of Margaret Thatcher as a vampire bat over the dartboard. Had it been any other politician, Tommy would have struggled to name them. But times had changed. The kid who unerringly switched off the news the moment it was announced, had no trouble identifying that Shah Jehan was up for election in a contest that was only two days away.

The adventurers spat out the dregs of their black tea and departed. Haggis did not want to leave it too late before fixing a site for the night and the increasing reluctance of the checkpoint officials to let them pass had not gone unnoticed. Something appeared to be brewing in Gilgit. Heavily-clothed men, armed to the teeth, crouched behind rocks as the Bedford pulled on, eyeing its occupants ferociously. Overhead, army helicopters droned, making for the sound of thunder further north. In contrast, to their right, the serene peak of Nanga Parbat rose above them at 8400 metres, disdainful of the plots and conspiracies of the puny beings far below.

At Jaglot, only an hour's drive short of Gilgit, the military refused Haggis further passage. There were problems in the town, the headman declared blandly, and the adventurers' safety could not be guaranteed. It would be necessary to pitch the tents at the checkpoint and proceed the following morning. Reluctantly, Tommy and the gang piled out and began hammering their pegs into the surrounding stone.

What followed could principally be blamed on Nokkers. She'd been betraying of late, the adventurers had noticed, an almost kamikaze urge to flaunt herself in front of the local male population. At the last village, she'd deliberately yawned and stretched herself in the manner of a Hollywood siren in view of some two hundred highly aroused males. Aroused more with anger at her brazen behaviour and lack of shame than with lust. She'd been wearing that apologetic green vest again, the one that made her breasts look like runaway sacks of potatoes. She'd posed like that, her legs slightly apart, until Haggis dragged her aboard just as the first rock flew. One young boy, then another, reached down for ammunition. A stone rattled against one of the roof supports, causing Big Nick a nasty cut on the ricochet, as Haggis pulled away.

Before the last tent had been pitched, news had filtered back to the village that the promiscuous western girls had been halted at the checkpoint. The barrier lay less than two kilometres from its outskirts. As dusk began to set in, a thick body of chanting men approached the encampment. They were half running, churning up a discernible fog from the dust and debris beneath them.

The military looked worried. Two young men, their eyes flickering with fear, were sent to intercede. One fingered a rifle, the other patted a club nervously into a cupped, greasy palm. Inside the hut that stood beside the checkpoint, the neatly moustached commander adjusted his beret slightly and distributed rifles to his two remaining men. Cap and Haggis had shepherded the adventurers into their tents. They then returned to the Bedford and assumed the crash position.

It was Tommy who saved the day. Tommy, with a little help from Marc-Marc. As adventurers everywhere scraped survival kits together and checked and rechecked the blades of clasp knives, Tommy struggled into his United strip. He'd brought his away kit too but something made him stick with the familiar. He pulled on the red shirt, leaving it loose over white shorts, and reached for his dark socks. There were no clear thoughts in his head as he did this. Outside, the clamour had reached fever pitch. Stones were whistling through the air and pocking the sides of the canvas. He seemed not to hear them. Maybe, just maybe, a psychologist would have said, he was like a man preparing to die and he wanted to be dressed in a way to be remembered. When they recorded the event in the *Manchester Evening News* or maybe in *The Pink,* the sports edition that came out on Saturday night, they'd describe the body and they'd know what had been important in Tommy's life. He juggled fleetingly with the prospect of his body being bludgeoned so badly that the undertakers down the road in Stretford might be forced to peel away the sticky remains of his United strip and deck him out afresh. 'Kit him out in footie gear,' Jog might say to Harry the Box, wiping a tear from his eye. Fine. But what if Harry the Box was a City fan? The prospect of Flegg and Grobbo coming to pay their last respects, peering over the lid, and finding him in a sky blue strip was unbearable.

Haggis used to keep the football in the cab but since it was Tommy who used it most it had now found a new home. Oblivious to the missiles whacking through the air, Tommy unzipped his tent and was away before Blondie had time to stop him. He strode towards Marc-Marc's site, the ball under his arm, like a referee who will stand for no nonsense, and as he did so the clamour abated.

Normally, Tommy would have knelt down and conducted the conversation face to face. On this occasion, he stood erect and called out thinly, his eye fixed on the canvas slopes.

98

'Fancy coming out for a kick around, Marc?'

The noise subsided completely now, washed away like tumbling rocks down a stream at this totally unforeseen turn in the proceedings.

'Tommy?' Marc-Marc's voice sounded strained, barely recognisable. 'Tommy?'

'Get your gear on. I'll be over by the road.' Tommy turned and dropped the ball to his left foot. He trapped it perfectly before it hit the ground and knocked it up in the air. To waist height. And trapped it with his right, plonking it forward slightly this time, controlling with the left.

'Tommy? Tommy? What are you doing, sweetheart?' Poppy was struggling desperately with the zipper of her tent. Cap was already out of his, as were Werner and Marc-Marc.

Slowly, methodically, Tommy advanced on the rifled throng, intense in his concentration.

'Twenty, Twenty one.' He shifted the ball to his left, tapped it up to knee height and then knocked it above his head.

'Twenty two, twenty three, twenty four.'

Behind him, an uneasy crescent of adventurers looked on, impotent players in a Greek chorus. He was past the military now, juggling between them, his forehead glued with dust and perspiration.

'Twenty five,' a voice called from the thick of the perplexed band in front of him. Tommy caught the ball as it dropped and grinned roguishly at a young man in a Miami Dolphins sweatshirt. He pointed accusingly at Tommy's red-and-white strip and then his bronzed face creased wide. 'Bow-bee Charlton.'

From behind, a hefty giant with ammunition belts strapped across his chest barged his way forward in an attempt to fathom this spindly phenomenon in red.

99

'Joe-gee Bess,' someone shouted from the throng. 'No-bee Style.'

Their burly leader cut the calls short with a fierce roar and a single shot from his antique firearm. It was discharged harmlessly into the air, causing a couple of hawks to wing for safety although they'd been well out of range. He shook his head fiercely in disapproval and jabbed his finger at Tommy's chest.

Tommy stood before him, a few days short of his fourteenth birthday now, his thin frame quaking. His retreating shock of ginger hair looked as if it were straining to leave his pale face.

The mountain man stared down at him and then roared again at the bristling band behind. Saliva flew from his wet lips, lodging itself on Tommy's chest.

'No No-bee Style,' he thundered, poking vigorously at Tommy's chest. 'Gorgon Strike-on. Mid-feel Maestro.'

A chorus of dissent rose from behind.

'No Gorgon Strike-on,' the young man who had opened the proceedings countered. 'Fair-kluff. Sooper slob.'

'Fancy a game?' Tommy seized the moment, glancing to his left. Marc-Marc stood there, his knees knocking. 'Me and Marc against you and you and . . .'

Cap turned to Jenny. 'Just tell Nokkers to stay out of sight till the morning. Tell her, if she was my daughter, I'd give her a good hiding. And if I see her wearing that vest again, I'll bloody burn it!' He fixed a genial smile on his face and strode forward, offering his services in goal.

According to the brochure, it should have been one hour's steady drive to Gilgit town. He didn't waste time but it still took Haggis more than double that before he pulled over in the shuttered market square.

Nothing was open. Rusted blue shutters, padlocked to bolts in concrete bases, hid merchants' goods from view.

100

Several proprietors stood defiantly in front of their stores, accompanied by a number of hefty cousins twiddling sticks. Knots of riot police lounged at every corner, their visors thrown back temporarily. Around the market square, restless, dark-eyed men swarmed, their numbers swelling by the minute as putting Suzukis swerved into sight and disgorged their rebellious cargoes.

Tommy leaned over to a drawn-looking Blondie. 'Looks like they've heard about Nokkers.'

Nokkers, in fact, on Haggis's instructions, had been strapped down in the least conspicuous part of the truck and forced to don one of Big Nick's many shapeless jumpers. In its best interests, the group had decided to disguise Nokkers' natural protuberances for a day or so; probably until the elections were over. Haggis allowed the adventurers an eyeful of the gladiatorial scene about to be enacted before veering away sharply in the direction of the fortified Tourist Lodge.

Drawing up before its battlements, Haggis eased out of the cab. 'Ah, ye c'n see who it is. The toon's closed up.' He had this almost schizophrenic tendency, when he was frightened or drunk, to shift into mad jock mode. The fearsome Scotsman swinging a cat round by its tail before spiking it down on the railings outside the hot, rank pubs of Easterhouse. 'It's up tae you who ye spen' the die. Personally, ah wouldnae advees goin' anywheres near the centre unless you want yer heid crackt.'

The option fell between remaining inside the perimeter wire of the lodge, eating fortified cornflakes for breakfast, or chartering a Suzuki up to the Hunza for a few hours. The Hunza, which began just north of Gilgit, was renowned for its sprightly centagenarians, many of whom knocked up to 130 before being cleanbowled of life. An abundant and fertile region, it could be negotiated in a few hours, though not by truck. The uncertain road, with its razorbacks and dizzy drops and rockfalls, offered passage to small vehicles only at selected times of the year.

Tommy and Poppy, the Australian family, Pinny and the Bolsterleys decided to commandeer a Suzuki. It was recruited with military efficiency on the strict understanding that its cargo would be returned by 4.30p.m. on the dot. Cap inspected the vehicle for defective parts but found none. It was no better, no worse, than the hundred or so other three-wheelers putt-putting for trade around the town. That is to say, its tyres were completely bald and there was no spare whilst the brakes had an excellent chance of functioning so long as the stopping distance was uphill and in excess of three hundred metres.

The journey up the valley proved breathtaking. To the east, the mighty peaks of Rakaposhi never left their view; to the west, below them, the turquoise waters of the Hunza raced. In the valley itself, a fertile, wonderfully silent place, autumnal colours were beginning to appear. The driver tricked and teased his machine as far as Ganish beyond which, he claimed, no westerner might travel. It had taken three hours and ahead of them lay China.

Although half the time allocated had disappeared, their slog had been uphill and the adventurers reasoned that the return trip would be a breeze. They calculated that they could just squeeze thirty minutes for lunch. The driver knew of a clean and well-appointed lodge and within minutes an order had been despatched. Gazing over a valley ablaze with autumn, they awaited the plat du jour: omelette, bread, potatoes, spinach and as many of the twenty varieties of apricot that grew there as could be assembled.

Tommy and Poppy fell into conversation with a PIA official lunching at the next table with his small child. Was it true, Poppy asked, about the phenomenal age ascribed to the inhabitants of the Hunza?

'Before my parents died, yes, it was true.' The father paused for a moment to adjust his glasses, searching for the diplomatic explanation. 'Until that time, my people were entirely self-sufficient. We lacked for nothing. We grew our food and made our clothes. There was no crime or theft, like now.' A pleasant smile on his face broadened as he continued. 'There was no telephone. If we wished to communicate with a friend across the valley, we shouted. Yes, shouted. In 1974, Bhutto's government annexed Hunza and immediately it began to tax us. It taxed our lands, our trade and all we produced. Our revenue and our wealth was drained away. But the one thing his inspectors forgot was the shouting. They taxed everything, apart from that.'

Tommy glanced at his watch. The time Cap had allowed for lunch had passed. No delicious kitchen smells were wafting through the mountain air.

'It was the beginning of the end, really. They built roads and destroyed our self-sufficiency. Outsiders came in, from the plains, carrying cartons of cigarettes and sacks of sugar. Travellers like yourselves introduced us to influenza. And now we die at the same age as your relatives in London and Adelaide.'

He leaned back on his solid, upright chair, made by village craftsmen well before annexation, and flicked open a pack of Salem. 'But at least I smoke menthol cigarettes.' He gazed from the verandah across the valley to the russet and copperclad hills beyond. 'Menthol for the mountain freshness. Isn't that what they say in the advertisements in England?'

Tommy gazed over in the direction of Rakaposhi but the mist had shrouded it from view.

For two days after their return, the clouds chased them

down the mountains. Storms of terrifying proportions blew up, provoking landslips and transforming roads into rivers in stretches they had just vacated. Overhead, a steady stream of military helicopters droned towards Gilgit. During the late afternoon and early evening the dull sound of gunfire merged with that of the thunder until it became impossible to say which was which.

Tommy's final image of Pakistan before crossing the border into India was of a seemingly endless line of coolies decked in orange robes. Each bore a weighty sack on his back which was dumped onto a blue Indian shoulder at the actual dividing-line between the countries. In the distance, Tommy could detect an unbroken blue line moving with the determination of ants towards Amritsar.

8

STARS OF INDIA

After weeks in Islam, the adventurers found themselves jolted by life over the border. The Indian Punjab, heartland of the Sikhs, proved to have clearly-defined plots of land that were well fertilised and cultivated. There was a buzz of energy about the place, in the fields, in the cottage industries and in the streets. Burly Sikh engineers set up a cacophonous racket from a nest of family workshops whilst their unveiled women zipped about bearing messages on motorised scooters. Old Nick, the theology student, explained that hard work is one of the tenets of Sikh philosophy. 'No room for idleness is one of their creeds. If they don't have a job, they help the needy or work for the community.'

Although it was probably for the best, Haggis scuppered the group's plans for a full day's sightseeing. Terrorist activity had been rampant in the province for weeks and most of it had centred on Amritsar. Trains had been derailed, buses ambushed and scores of innocent Hindus killed. The root of the problem lay in the Sikhs' vision of Khalistan, an independent state to be carved out of the Punjab. Negotiations with the government had proved to be fruitless, they claimed, and now the time had come for violent action. Haggis suggested a stopover of two hours before the mortars went off.

By early afternoon the group was on the outskirts of

the city, heading for Kashmir. In terms of accommodation, what lay ahead was probably the luxury highlight of the trip. The company had hired two magnificent houseboats, extravagant relics from the Raj, for five days. They lay permanently moored on the far side of Lake Dal, the still, beautiful stretch of water which formed a crescent around the region's capital, Srinegar. A sumptuous suite had been assigned to each couple with servants on hand to cater for their slightest whim. After two months' scuffling around, almost a week of reckless self-indulgence awaited the adventurers.

Eventually, the even plains of the Punjab fell away to thick, forested wedges as the truck made its second gradual ascent into the Great Himalayan Range. Chunky, triangular folds replaced the wedges as Haggis began to negotiate the highways of Jammu. The population became less dense, although truckstops never failed to draw a crowd, usually of skinny, wide-eyed kids. Unlike the Moslems, the adventurers noticed, the Hindus tended to keep a greater distance, though there was the same fascination with every movement. They watched the setting up of trestle tables with interest, the preparation and consumption of food with absorption and the placing on one side of leftovers with a total and absolute concentration. As the truck pulled away, the audience's self-control would snap and excited groups would surge forward to scour the vacated area for scraps of food and dropped peanuts.

It was somewhere in Jammu that Tommy spotted the first of what became a rash of warning signs. Poppy deduced that the local council must be overrun with failed poets:

CARELESS DRIVERS KILL AND DIE
LEAVING KITH AND KIN TO CRY

They were standard features on the hairpin bends and

106

it rapidly became a competition to spot a fresh one:

ALWAYS ALERT, ACCIDENT AVERT
DO NOT BE RASH AND END IN A CRASH

When they couldn't find one, they made them up, highlighting each other as they went along:

DRIVER, DRIVER, DO NOT DALLY
EXIT LEFT, HERE COMES SALLY

CAUTIOUS DRIVER, WATCH FOR WERNER
HE IS WORSE THAN ANY LEARNER

Annoyingly, there was little to rhyme with 'Haggis', and it took Tommy, in a rare moment of poetic flight, to lampoon the oblivious Scot in the cab:

ON THIS TRIP THE ONLY SNAG IS
BEING IN THE CAB WITH HAGGIS

Everybody's favourite, though, came as they were leaving the region, betraying as it did the main reason for the spate of accidents along the highway:

DARLING, DO NOT NAG
WHILST I AM NEGOTIATING CURVE

'There's one for yer old man, Pom,' Nokkers smiled. 'Turn it into a car sticker.' Tommy thought back to the fading legend on their back windscreen: FOLLOW ME AND MANCHESTER UNITED. He seemed to have dredged it up from a different lifetime.

As the truck's ascent continued through forests of rising conifers, the air became noticeably sharper. Monkeys chattered and parrots screeched in the surrounding trees. The villages and small towns became more colonial in character, being almost entirely given over to verandahed bungalows with red corrugated roofs. Cap reminded Tommy that this was where the Brits came during the hot season to escape the intensity of the plains.

They spent the night in Banihal, camping outside a line of attractive tourist bungalows. Further down was the

Roxy Bar, dispenser of Rosy Pelican beer and over a hundred varieties of whisky. Tommy settled down to write a few cards, leaving Blondie to listen to the proprietor's complaints of administrative bumbledom and get quietly sozzled.

When he returned to the bungalows, all hell appeared to have been let loose. Two coaches had pulled in, hours behind schedule, packed with disgruntled Hindus. In seconds, the place was in uproar, as they swarmed over the luggage bays and fought over sleeping space. Tommy glanced with interest at the logo emblazoned across the side of each coach. It was unusual to see wealthy Hindus on tour. At first, he thought the froth from Blondie's Rosy Pelican was playing tricks on his vision but he looked again and there it was: 'PANICKERS' TRAVEL. Haggis sidled up beside him and breathed beery fumes into his ear. 'Did yer know they were a subsidiary of Coffin Tours?' Tommy thought back to the casket-shaped tourist transporters he had seen in Syria, loaded with cardiac cases from the Ruhr, but there was no time to question whether he was serious, for Haggis had lumbered off into the gloom.

Less then forty eight hours later, the Bedford burst through the Jawarhar Tunnel into the Vale of Kashmir. Lingering greens mingled with the rust of autumn on the valley floor. Future cricket bats and silver birch predominated though large, purple-tinged areas caught Tommy's eye from time to time. The saffron crop was being harvested. Dozens of valley farmers and their families were bent double, laboriously plucking the valued strands from the stamens of the purple flower.

The houses were an interesting blend of the Himalayan and the colonial, though rather drab in appearance. Haggis pulled over at a chai house in Pampori, fourteen kilometres short of their destination. He'd wanted to make a few things clear about procedures on the house boats but Cap was clearly bursting with curiosity about an entirely different matter and he got in first.

'Hey, Haggis! Why do all the guys look pregnant?'

Tommy glanced around, first at the heavily garbed denizens of the chai house and then at their brethren outside. It was true. Each one wore a dark thickly woven cape from which protruded a telltale hump.

Haggis lurched over to a black-toothed individual crouching by the stove. Smiling and gesturing by way of explanation, he pulled aside the thick folds of the man's cape. Inside hung a wire basket, like a small bird cage, steaming with its precious contents: a pot of hot ashes. 'That, ladies and gentleman,' Haggis enunciated in his poshest tour guide tones, 'is a *kangri,* more commonly known as a hot water bottle. Welcome to the Land of the False Pregnancy.'

Their approach into Srinegar, Kashmir's capital, reduced the adventurers into awed silence. Even Werner, as he chomped and champed upon his charcoal, said nothing. A sight that would have held Tommy's attention for a few seconds before the summer now held him entranced. Before the summer, if it didn't have goal posts, it wasn't worth looking at. He didn't seem to think that way any more. *Shikara* boys paddled the adventurers from the jetties of the town across the still waters of Lake Dal to where their floating palaces awaited them. Tommy's *shikara* cut on relentlessly, hissing through the water like a snake beyond *Miss America* and *Soul Kiss.* It slid gently to the wharf of the *Aristotle* where a knot of adventurers, including the Granites, was permitted to disembark.

Passing from its intricately carved balcony, Tommy drifted into the reception room, a spacious, sumptuous chamber lit by glittering chandeliers. Rich carpets lay scattered across its floors whilst elegant suites of oriental design were dotted almost carelessly about their borders. All heating emanated from the centrally placed stove, in front of which Noonda and his houseboys stood.

'It is my pleasure to welcome you aboard *Aristotle*.' Noonda flashed his dark Kashmiri eyes, bowing slightly as he spoke. 'I hope your stay will be a happy and restful one.'

Behind him, through the chinks in the carved wood screen, Tommy could glimpse a dining area. The table had been set immaculately for twelve, with starched white napkins and silver service cutlery. Three mini chandeliers hung above it, bathing the area in soft, yellow light.

Later, over the dining table, Cap began talking about his years as a supermarket manager. His shop worked on a profit of only one per cent on turnover. That meant that shoplifting caused a severe dent in company funds and thieves had to be dealt with punitively in order to discourage others.

Haggis now took up the topic, weighing in with his own experiences in the thick brogue he unleashed when either drunk or violent. Tommy had had a sneak preview in Noonda's honesty book and recorded that it was undisputedly the former; Haggis had knocked back sixteen beers since early afternoon.

'Aye. I was a supermarket manager once, doon the Easter Road.' There followed a brief but graphic description of Glasgow's battlefield precinct of broken bottles and blood. 'Hell of a place. Used tae hae it like a bluidy fortress tae stop 'em liftin'.'

Tommy sank back into his armchair. There was no doubt that Haggis could tell a good story.

'It's one wet Saturday afternoon and ah'm in mah office lookin' through one o' those two-way gizmos at the punters. Ah can see them, like, but they canna see me.' He paused, wetting his lips with obvious relish. 'Anyway, in walks these three geezers, really heavy lads, straight oot the pubs. Ah could smell the whisky on them through the bluidy glass. They walks up tae the meat 'n' dairy reet below mah winder an' start stuffin' the gear under their coats. Ah looks roond an' there's no an assistant in sight. They're all hidin' behind the bluidy dog food. Ah'm breakin' out in a cold sweat but ah'm the manager an' it's up tae me tae stop 'em. "HEY, YOU!" ah yell, in this booming invisible voice, "PUT THE BLUIDY MEAT BACK!"' Haggis paused to rattle the heat control of the stove. 'These lads wondered what the hell had hit 'em. They could hear me but they couldna bluidy see me. So they puts the meat back and makes to go. "AND THE BLUIDY BUTTER!" ah yell. Oot comes the butter from under their coats. They're heavy lads these, but they're gettin' panicky. Perhaps they think it's God. Anyway, they're lookin' this way an' that, up an' doon the aisles, an' eventually one bawls, "Excuse me, mister. Hoo do we get oot?" "IF AH CATCH YOU IN HERE AGAIN," ah yell, "IT'LL BE THROUGH THE BLUIDY WINDER!" Ah'm really gettin' intae it noo. These guys dodge oot, really petrified, past the checkout. They get tae the door an' turn. "BASTARD!" one yells, they all flick V-signs an' then go hoofin' doon the rood.'

Haggis sank back in satisfaction at a tale well told. 'Ah tell ya, ah can laugh noo but ah was bluidy scared at the time.'

Seemingly from nowhere, Noonda appeared, pulling on a hubble-bubble pipe.

'Hey, I've got some stuff to put in that,' Nokkers burst out, to the general astonishment of all. She delved into her traveller's bag and rooted out a dark, pliable ball of hashish. Noonda held out his hand to examine it, turning

111

the drug over and sniffing like a dog.

'Third grade stuff, missy,' he announced. 'No good.'

'Aw, Nooon-da,' Nokkers coaxed. 'C'mon, bang it in.'

As she inhaled for the third time, Cap rose and tapped his daughter on the shoulder. Alison had been half-listening to Haggis but her guilty gaze had been focused on the stove. 'C'mon, Allie. Time to turn in.' She looked up to remonstrate but there was no mistaking the firmness of Cap's expression. There was no room for negotiation there. She gathered her things and left the room with her lips tight.

'Oooh. Is this something special? Can anybody have a try?' Poppy bent over the hubbly-bubbly and inhaled deeply. 'Gorg-eous,' she intoned. 'What a wonderful aroma!' Nokkers rolled her head back and passed up the pipe. Tommy, somewhat mystified, slouched in the corner and said nothing.

'So after she's put all the stuff back on the shelves, she swaggers over, undoin' the top button of her dress, like. "AH'M LOOKIN' FOR A MAN WITH AN EIGHT-INCH COCK," she yells, tryin' tae humiliate me in front o' the punters. "IS THERE ANY POINT ME SEEIN' YER TONIGHT AFTER THE SHOP CLOSES?" "THERE'S NAE POINT, DARLIN'," ah roar back, makin' sure everyone in Easter Road gets an earful, "COS AH'M NOT CUTTIN' MAH COCK IN HALF FER ANY-BODY!"'

The adventurers fell back laughing, especially Werner, whose grasp of Scottish gutter language never failed to impress Tommy.

'So she comes over, determined not to be outdone, like, an' whispers in mah ear. "What you've seen today is nothin', boy," she says, "it's the tip o' the biggest iceberg in yer imagination."'

The adventurers nodded sagely. Noonda, Tommy

noticed, had long ceased to pull on the hubble-bubble. Nokkers had been sucking at it with an increasing listlessness for about ten minutes, although Poppy was still going at it energetically.

A tidal wave of sound from the neighbouring boat suddenly washed about the *Aristotle*'s lounge, tearing the adventurers from their reveries. All afternoon, a gentle, uninterrupted rhythm of young voices had been spreading across the waters but now it burst like a giant breaker. The powerful lungs of at least a dozen men, backed by an exuberant Kashmiri band, reverberated through the walls. Noonda explained that October was the month of weddings and that festivities would continue for a week. The marriage aboard *Soul Kiss* was destined to take place in two days' time.

Nokkers had by now keeled onto her back and was lying, knees bent in the air, staring at the ceiling with a stunned, unbroken gaze. Tommy was reminded of the time he had whipped a cloth off his budgie's cage one morning and found it adopting a similar position on its sheet of grit.

And then Werner was bubbling in the doorway with a slender Kashmiri behind him. 'We are all invited,' he growled happily, beckoning the company to troop along behind him. 'They are making Kashmiri music.'

Tommy lingered solicitously for a moment, concerned that Nokkers should not go the way of his dead budgie. 'I'm okay, you guys', she intoned hollowly. 'Catch you later.'

Poppy sprang up with the others and made for the door.

'Whooooo!' she shrieked, as a blast of cool air rose off the lake to greet her. 'I hope everybody's ready to dance.' She pranced along the wooden jetty, flicking her thin skirt to the heavens as she skipped. 'La la, la Bamba.

Bom bom bom, bom, bom, bom. La la, la Bamba!'

Perplexed, Tommy turned to Marc-Marc. 'What's wrong with her, Marc? Why is she acting like she's drunk?' He turned to catch her, toes curled over the last available piece of planking. Poppy was still fully dressed but she'd adopted the stance of a high board diver.

'They call my baby La Bamba. Is anybody coming in?'

Marc-Marc moved to catch her but Poppy had already gone. She hit the water, arms outstretched, in a perfect belly-flop, as the adventurers drew round.

'Whoooo!' Poppy's bobbing head was thrown back and her eyes were shining. 'Come on in! The water's lovely. Whoooo!'

The wedding took place the following day. Until the sun set, women sang and children chanted. And then, with several hundred people packed aboard *Soul Kiss,* the fireworks began. As they flared and crashed across a clear sky, a line of *shikaras* set off from the opposite shore. The first to butt across the gentle waters bore a bagpipe band whose task it was to pipe aboard the groom. He, Noonda explained, would be on the very last *shikara* to arrive.

As this final vessel nudged into view with its precious cargo, the revels erupted. Every square inch of floor space on every houseboat was occupied by stamping, screaming Kashmiris. Along the wharf, demented bag-pipers wailed as a constant fizz of fireworks sprang cracking into the night sky. The groom, an ashen young man of twenty six, had to be assisted from his *shikara* to a more solid footing. Ushers with vice-like arms took him by the shoulder and hoisted his limp flesh to the wooden planking. Noonda explained that the groom had good reason to be fearful; he had yet to cast his eyes on his wife. With banknotes, according to Kashmiri tradition, pinned liberally across his chest, the young man was dragged inside to the accompaniment of the crazed pipers.

Fate, however, seemed to rule with an aberrant hand in the Himalayas. The morning after the wedding party, Noonda interrupted Poppy's singing to announce gloomily that the bride was already a widow. The celebrations had continued until midnight, at which point the guests had departed and the honeymoon commenced. By twelve twenty, the groom had expired, seemingly of some massive shock to his system.

Death's shadow seemed to have stalked the adventurers, settling about their perimeters, and as their luxury stay wore on it showed little sign of receding. It was during the evening prior to departure that Poppy noticed Noonda performing his duties with all the zeal of a man awaiting execution. He served dinner listlessly and collected their plates with neither energy nor charm. When she had a moment, Poppy took Noonda to one side. 'Is something troubling you?' she enquired, with genuine concern.

The little Kashmiri gazed downwards and fixed his attention on an insignificant stain on the carpet. He wore jeans and a leather bomber in the manner of westernised Kashmiris but his dark eyes and complexion made his features indistinguishable from those of any street vendor in the town.

'Oh, madam. I am not a lucky man.'

Noonda had gone beyond the temptation of many Kashmiri boys to ape their western guests, sucked into the delusion that material possessions and loose behaviour are desirable proofs of a superior culture. He had dashed all plans for his arranged marriage at the eleventh hour, falling under the spell of a siren from Frankfurt.

'For three months, madam, we live as man and wife,' Noonda continued. 'She returns to Germany and I am to

115

follow her when the paperwork is complete. Today, from my friend, I hear that she is dead.'

Poppy found herself appalled by this blight which seemed to strike Kashmiris of a marriageable age.

'But how do you know this is the truth?'

Noonda's face became streaked with thick, salty channels.

'Because, madam, her parents write to me at my village. My friend opens the letter and telephones me.'

Poppy scraped around for questions that might test Noonda's certainty.

'Was she involved in a traffic accident?'

'No, madam. She died in a restaurant with four friends. Her food was poisoned.' Noonda shook with grief. 'The police are investigating. Her parents have promised to write to me after the funeral.'

There was little Poppy felt she could do. She composed and posted a letter to the dead girl's parents on Noonda's behalf, attempting to express the grief of the little Kashmiri. And when, on the following morning, it was time to bid goodbye, she dug more deeply into her pocket than she intended and pressed a banknote of sizeable proportions into Noonda's hand.

The houseboy's tragedy went unmentioned until Haggis had backtracked out of the valley. Poppy, deep in thought, had sat beside him in the cab, along with Blondie, until the truck had burst into light at the far end of the Jawarhar Tunnel. 'Do you want to hear the saddest of stories?' she wondered, still dewy-eyed. Haggis and Blondie eased themselves back into their seats. They had eight hours to kill. Poppy's domestic tragedy took but a fraction of their time.

'The scheming bitch!' Blondie coughed it out and it was difficult to tell whether he was choking with rage or admiration. 'So out she comes from Deutschland, hot for experiences, and thinks how hip it would be to shack up with a local boy by the lake. Sort of primitive cool.' Blondie scratched his whiskers and emitted a second ambiguous bark. 'She makes all kinds of promises to seduce the kid. Not just his body; she wants to do his head in as well. Liberate him from the chains of Islam. When the buzz goes, she quits. Catches her flight back to civilisation, boasts about her far out trip and gets one of her girlfriends to fake a letter back to Kashmir. Probably does it over a lager outside some pavement cafe. Stops Noonda pestering her.' Poppy caught the expression on Blondie's face in the cab mirror and the intensity of its malevolence startled her. 'Pretty neat trick. Sort of thing I might pull myself. She's probably being rooted by some black Yank on an airforce base right now, en route to her next experience. Whaddya reckon, Hag?'

Haggis smiled. 'Heard it before.'

Poppy was astonished. 'What! You mean, he told you too . . .'

Haggis brushed aside the question and posed one of his own. 'How much did you tip him?' Poppy stuttered out an answer. 'Aye. That's what he was after. You've been had, Pop.' Blondie leaned back and stroked his beard in admiration.

Beyond the Jawarhar Tunnel, there was little cause for map-reading. To get to Delhi, Haggis simply pointed the truck in a southerly direction and let it roll downhill. Twenty four hours later they were ghosting through the Punjab, seemingly invisible to the toiling communities thrown up on either side of the highway. Sikhs, glossy with sweat, bent their muscular bodies in a sprawl of sawmills and foundries, oblivious to the glazed eyes of the westerners drifting by. Improvised food stalls proliferated and there was little point adhering to the three-meals-a-day plan that the adventurers had exported from the west. They just stopped when they were hungry and nibbled at local tidbits. Tommy bought a couple of lightly fried vegetable samosas, packed with chick peas and grandly wrapped in a ragged page of school exercise paper. Fogged by memories of a past routine, he peered at the pencilled writing. It was neat and accurately presented. A number of generous, looping ticks in red biro were splashed appreciatively across the page. It appeared to be an assignmnent on the Battle of Waterloo.

Cap leaned over his shoulder to pick at an inviting chickpea and to make a sly observation of the script. There was no doubt it was a damn sight neater than anything that anybody in Tommy's class could produce.

'Now that's what I call recycling. Didja know that the average western kid consumes one hundred and twenty five times as much paper and packaging as a kid from a developing country?'

Cap's 'didja knows' were invariably moralistic but Tommy had become increasingly fascinated by them. He thought back to the Macdonald's cartons and the tubs of Kentucky Fried Chicken which littered the streets. He thought back to the casual way in which he and his mates used exercise books, scribbling and scrawling on them and throwing them laughingly across each others' lockers. If you lost your book, you just forked out 20p. for a new one. End of story.

'Mind you, you Brits could be worse,' Cap continued. 'The average American household uses up in one day the amount of trash it takes a Pom household a fortnight to accumulate.'

'Does somebody buy you books on this sort of thing for Christmas?' Tommy joked but Cap's point had lodged firmly in place.

'It's a lot of oil . . .'

118

'An' a lot of trees. I know.' Tommy thought fleetingly of a year's supply of junk mail, a mountain of trash heaped on the hall carpet. It would probably prove impossible for Jog to step over it. He'd need a ladder. He thought too about Flegg and Grobbo. If he wrote to them about stuff like this, they'd think he was nuts.

'Gis a bit, Tommy.' Books stood behind him, sniffing hopefully at his samosas. Tommy raised an arm backwards, proffering a corner of his lunch. Books' whale-like mouth engulfed not only the entire samosa but a portion of his finger. She swallowed greedily, not stopping to chew, thoughtfully pushing Tommy's flesh back into the open air with her tongue. 'Ten of those, please,' she breathed to the astonished samosa salesman, as a recalcitrant piece of chickpea lodged itself in one of the fatty hollows of her oesophagus. 'They're not all for me,' she countered, catching Tommy's blank look. 'One of them's for Pinny.'

Delhi was a city aswirl with sorcery. They crept in under a fat, yellow moon and succumbed immediately to its spell. Flaring hurricane lamps swung hypnotically from flanking stalls heaped with bulbous helmets; filthy, ancient crones squatted in the dirt below, hawking fruit; legless beggars quanted by on low trolleys and lines of Sikhs queued expressionlessly outside liquor stores. Beside the tourist camp, a tintambulating Hare Krishna convention shed warm, golden light on all the surrounding neighbourhood. Its thousands of devotees glowed in a vast, collective aura as they poured their eulogies into the night sky.

'Think of a flower, sir.' The rheumy-eyed mystic blocking Tommy's path somehow caused all extraneous sounds to filter out, leaving the adventurer to concentrate on the beggarly figure before him. The curves and folds of the man's white dhoti could not disguise his spindliness. He stooped so that Tommy did not have to crane his neck back too far to make eye contact. 'Any flower, sir.'

The man was patently a magician. White strips of cloth had been woven about his head in a vain struggle to temper his wild demeanour. His tangled beard and locks were a writhing basket of snakes and his eyes blazed with preternatural power. An Old Testament prophet, left baking in the desert for 2000 years.

Tommy grinned, a little uncomfortably. 'Oh, chrysanthemum,' he answered evenly.

The madman smiled, wolf-like, and slowly unclasped his left palm. He had been holding it high, close to Tommy's shoulder, in an attempt to deny him passage. His fingers unfolded slowly until they were perhaps two inches from his thumb. A small business card formed a wafer-like bridge between them and on it was written CHRYSANTHEMUM.

'And now, madam, I will ask you to think of a plant.'

'Rubber plant,' Poppy intoned automatically, as if she were playing a word association game in the parlour back home. The Indian unclenched his right fist, revealing a second card to the rapidly paling Poppy. Not for a second did he allow his bloody gaze on Tommy to become unfixed.

'I have the name of your mother.' He leaned into Tommy's ear and mouthed a word of two syllables. 'And your grandmother's, although she, of course, is dead now.' The magician smiled grimly. 'But these things you know. They belong to your past.' He raised himself to his full height and placed a fizzing hand on each of the Granite's shoulders. Even through their T-shirts, it was like receiving a mild electric shock. 'Give me 150 rupees and we will talk of your future.'

Back at the camp, Cap was haranguing a beerbelly

from Oregon on the evils of colonialism.

'We were no better than the Brits,' he confided. 'Did you ever hear of the Van Dieman's Land Stock Company?' Beerbelly shook his head dumbly. 'Ever hear of Tasmania?' Another shake. 'Well, this company operated in Tazzy and it was responsible for wiping out one complete strand of Aborigines, a particularly creative and industrious tribe.' Cap paused to catch the man's eye and he held his gaze in what seemed to Tommy to be a tangible shaft of steely light. 'The company's employees went out in shooting parties every Sunday, hunting the Abos down for sport. Like animals.'

In most of the adventurers' minds, Delhi was the last real staging post before the group broke up in Kathmandu. There were intermediary stops planned, of course, but as the truck pulled out of the city a sense of finality began to creep in. Within days, the Asian Assault Course would, for some, be over. Several of the British girls were flying straight home from Kathmandu, taking their views of the Himalayas from the panorama afforded by the window seats of their aircraft. Others were continuing into South-east Asia, plotting downwards towards Oz. The Granites, in company with a handful of others, intended to rest up in Kathmandu for a spell before joining an expedition to the hills. It wouldn't take long, maybe three weeks. After that, they could take their ease in one of the town's 132 pie shops, massage their blisters and contemplate their futures.

Haggis's route to the Himalayas was by way of Amber and Jaipur, Agra and Khajaraho. Unwisely, Tommy clambered into the cab, ill-prepared for Haggis's appalling repertoire of racist jokes, a dubious cabaret that was only thrown off course when the Scot swerved to avoid one of the many abandoned wrecks rusting by the wayside.

'So the Indian government,' Haggis opens, 'looks at the successes of the marathons in London and New York and it decides to stage a national marathon of its own.' He wrenched the wheel violently out of the path of a juggernaut loaded with stinking fodder. 'To encourage entrants, it generously offers 100 rupees to each runner.' He braked suddenly as a cow strolled obliviously across the tarmac from behind an upturned bus some twenty metres ahead. As Tommy lurched forward, his forehead seemingly engaged in violent assault against the windscreen, he had time to notice villagers ripping straw padding from the seats of the abandoned bus. 'So when the entry papers come in, the government finds there's half a million blokes fancy their chances. And that's just in Delhi. Too many,' Haggis intones seriously. 'So one joker suggests that only men with one testicle should be eligible and fresh entry papers are distributed.' The road fell away as Haggis continued, leaving only one lane open for traffic. The Scot put his foot down and the Bedford roared on. In the distance, Tommy detected a petrol wagon hurtling towards them, the sun's rays reflecting off its curved tank. On either side, the roadworks continued with no end in sight.

'Christ! Think we'll make this okay?' Tommy breathed.

'Tek nae notice. It's jest a bluff.' Haggis sniffed. 'They come bombin' doon on yer like this, darin' yer tae carry on. It's a wee game, seein' whose first tae gie the way an' pull over. Where was ah wi' that joke?'

Tommy's brain had quickly been alerted to Haggis's gearstick change into Jockspeak. It signalled accelerated emotions, leaving common sense at the starting line. He noticed too that the road had now fallen away completely on one side. It had crumbled, at an angle of about sixty degrees, into a dried river bed lying alongside. To Tommy's left, a sheer cliff wall rose up, its top escaping the sight of the worried figure inside the cab.

The tanker was now 200 metres away and burning up the tarmac with demonic speed. Its headlamps and barred radiator grill gave it the facial appearance of some crazed metallic monster charging down on its defenceless lunch.

'One geezer,' Haggis continued, 'parked opposite me, bumper tae bumper, screen tae screen, for an hour and a half. We spent all that time trying tae psych each other out . . .'

'HAGGIS! HE'S NOT GOING TO STOP!' Tommy screamed, eyes rolling about his head. The nightmare on wheels was now about thirty metres away. Haggis pulled imperceptibly to his left, causing his wing mirror to scrape against the cliff face. The monster thundering up adjusted fractionally too and it sped by them belching oil and spitting gravel.

'We both had our ignitions off,' Haggis recalled, 'and then he pulls out this newspaper. Puts his feet up against the dash and buries his head in the cartoon page.' Tommy, bathed in sweat and with heart pumping, had sunk back into the luxury of his padded seat. His eyes were closed and he had ceased to listen.

Haggis jerked him awake as they approached Amber, ten kilometres or so from the pink city of Jaipur. It rose before them, the Maharajah's summer palace, a vast, walled, labyrinthine place long since given over to dogs and monkeys. Tommy purchased an assortment of nuts from an indifferent vendor and set off munching into a maze of yellow plaster stained with the grime of history.

He was surprised how quickly he lost all human contact. He traversed a substantial courtyard boasting jungly foliage and a pond of murky water and beyond that he was alone. Deserted passages and sad corridors swallowed him. Monkeys had long ceased to chatter in these quarters and the only sound came from his own muffled footfalls.

Abruptly, Tommy turned a corner and burst into sunlight. A brushed square lay before him, in the centre of which stood the Maharajah's harem. Lolling about its staircase were four young Hindus, smartly dressed and engaging in the upmarket chatter of local yuppies.

Catching sight of Tommy, they beckoned him over with undisguised glee.

'Welcome to our country, young sir.' One pumped his hand enthusiastically. 'You are from England, I think.'

Tommy nodded. 'That's right.' The movement caused his camera case to dangle lumpily against his side.

'We four are doctors, sir,' the spokesman continued. 'Newly moved to this city from southern India.' Tommy noticed that they were unusually dark in complexion.

'Postgraduates engaged in medical research,' the tubbiest chipped in bravely.

'What is your opinion of Amber Palace?' the confident one persisted. 'Have you seen the elephants?'

It was possible for tourists to take an elephant ride from the town of Amber to its palace gates.

'Yes. I saw the elephants.'

'And do you have elephants in England?'

Tommy shook his head and attempted to look downcast. Collectively, the doctors drew closer at this sudden revelation.

'But . . .' the spokesman continued aghast, 'You have seen the monkeys. Surely you have monkeys in England?'

Tommy thought back to the vendor of nuts at the palace entrance. The man had had to employ a pack of yapping hounds to keep the resident colony of monkeys from his merchandise. It appeared to be a constant battle to secure his stock. Monkeys came skipping nimbly down walls, swooping on the coloured piles from the man's stall and were away. Dogs chased them around, barking furiously, but the monkeys were too wily. On the flat, open spaces they knew the dogs had them beaten but when it came to lightning assaults from the battlements, they were untouchable. They operated, therefore, from above ground level, swooping down onto the dust for only a few seconds at a time. A variation of guerilla warfare.

'No,' he lamented, shaking his head sadly. 'We have no monkeys in England. Except,' he added as an afterthought, 'in the football team of Manchester City.'

'But they still get 100,000 applicants,' Haggis leered, slanting his eyes off the road towards a beaming Poppy. 'Which is still too much at 100 rupees an entrant.' Haggis paused to let the mathematical implications marinade in Poppy's brain as he pulled out on the road to Agra, the town that would have sunk in the mire without the imagination of Shah Jehan. 'So they decide to limit the entrants of the marathon to those who have had both bollocks removed.' He tucked in on the busy road behind a cranky blue bus that was belching oil and spewing gas.

'As you might gather, applications fell away to one half of a per cent of the last lot. Got that? 100,000 divided by 200. It came to a figure that the government found highly acceptable.' He glanced to his left, catching Poppy crossing noughts off with her fingers. He held off for a second or two, until Poppy had nearly got there, before delivering the punchline: 'And that's how the Indian-knackerless 500 came into being!'

He smirked into the cab mirror, catching Poppy's patient, if dulled, expression. 'Yes,' she said politely. 'And then . . .?' Haggis turned to the road ahead, his repertoire extinguished.

To the adventurers' surprise, he pulled over a few

kilometres short of Agra, turning at a dilapidated road sign for Fatehpur Sikri. 'Victory City,' he sniffed, and drew into the car park just down the road. 'Worth a visit,' he pouted, peering at the towers and battlements of the sixteenth century complex beyond. The adventurers piled out.

'Two types of guide,' Haggis informed them, nodding at a small band of officials squatting in the dust about the entrance. 'First class and second class. 20 rupees for the first, 14 for the second class. I'll see ya at the other end.'

As Haggis made off, one of the adventurers snagged him by the arm. 'Hold on, mate,' Nokkers grinned at him quizzically. 'What's the difference between 'em?'

Haggis pulled thoughtfully on the strands of ginger foliage that threatened to overwhelm his upper lip. 'The second class don't speak English.' He bit half-heartedly at one of the offending strands and mooched off.

'The city was built by Akbar on the advice of a local holy man,' the 20-rupee guide explained. 'Despite his four wives, two Hindu, a Christian and a Moslem, Akbar had not been blessed by a son.' Poppy broke away to admire the astonishing vista of parapets and brown towers. Ten kilometres of undulating city walls enclosed them. 'The holy man led Akbar to this place and promised one of his wives would conceive at this spot. Out of the wilderness, he built Fatehpur Sikri, home for half a million people. In 1568, Akbar took up residence and within one year was the proud father of Jehangir.'

Werner leaned over and nudged Tommy. 'Jehan's father, the guy who built the Taj.'

Tommy snorted. 'And Dad told me he was a squash player!'

'Seemingly,' the guide continued, in impeccable Oxbridge tones, 'the water supply ran out some years later and Fatehpur became deserted, almost overnight. Here

126

we see,' he pointed casually to a monument on his right, 'the tomb of the Justice Elephant. This animal, a favourite of Akbar's, would dine with him in the banqueting hall. Wrongdoers were laid below the elephant. If it refused three times to trample on them, they were declared innocent and released.'

Over on the far side of the city, the highest arch in Asia loomed. It marked the end of the guided tour and Haggis had promised to meet the adventurers there. Tommy, Blondie, Nokkers and a few of the others approached it simultaneously, gazing up at its Moghul splendour.

A wild, frothing old man brought them down to earth. He wore a soiled, ragged dhoti and his eyes rolled as he spat into his eighty-year-old beard. Ill-advisedly, he clutched and tugged at Blondie's exposed arm. 'Sir, sir, I am jumping wallah. Give me 20 rupees.' His spittle sprayed freely across Blondie's chest. 'Jumping-wallah, sir. Jumping-wallah. Give me 20 rupees.' Blondie's pupils dilated and he drew back his unhindered arm to deliver a blow which would have transported the old man to an infinitely more peaceful world.

'Excuse me, sir.' Tommy's 20-rupee guide interposed himself between the combatants like a well-meaning referee. 'Allow me to explain. This poor man,' he flicked a finger in the direction of the gibbering wreck before him, 'secures his living by leaping from the highest point of the battlement there into the lake.' He paused to indicate a miserable blob of water that could only charitably be described as a puddle. 'I can tell you, sir,' the guide shook his head sadly, 'it is not a happy living.'

Jumping-wallah had clearly been following his deliverer's case with interest and he adjudged that this fleeting moment of compassion was the time to strike. 'Give me 20 rupees!' he exhorted, tugging anew on Blondie's arm. The Aussie threw him off with a snarl and waggled his finger venomously at the guide.

'Tell him,' he breathed poisonously, 'that I'll give the bugger 50 rupees to jump from the battlements down to there.' He tipped his finger away from the puddle in the direction of a pile of hard core. 'Onto the bleedin' concrete, 50 rupees,' he emphasised, mouthing the words slowly so as there should be no mistake. Gleaming demonically, he pointed a finger to the ledge above the battlements and let it drop slowly onto the small pyramid of hard core. 'Fifty rupees.' Blondie held both hands up for the benefit of the old man and flashed them five times.

Jumping-wallah's eyes flickered, caught between fear and temptation, but Haggis was already in the cab and pipping the horn. Blondie was bundled in and the adventurers were swiftly away in a cloud of dust. They failed to hear the cries of the forlorn old man behind them: 'Okay, mister, okay. Give me 60 rupees.'

As they drew close to Agra, the customary banter and jokery subsided and the travellers applied themselves to the task of spotting the world's most famous monument. Haggis had advised them to visit the Taj Mahal as many times as possible in one day, as the changing intensity of the light wrought subtle changes in its beauty.

'It's not a case of "been there, done that" with the Taj,' he'd mumbled philosophically. 'There's something . . . spiritual about the place.' He seemed to have difficulty in forcing the word out.

The truck entered from the unfashionable side of town and Haggis spent forty five minutes nudging the Bedford through a teeming native market. There were no tourists in evidence until the adventurers had progressed to the well laid out, old colonial section of the town. As they picked up speed along its spacious avenues, curving in a wide arc around the boundaries of the golf course, Big Nick yelled out like a pirate in the rigging, 'There she is, across the water!'

The Taj stood gleaming in the distance, on the far side of a fat, lazy snake of water. The adventurers camped along The Mall, in the grounds of a somewhat gone-to-seed dak bungalow. They ate quickly, fired with the intention of making their first pilgrimage in time for sunset.

'Hi there, Mycock's the name. How's it going, guys?'

Tommy and Books lay sprawled across the lawns in the shadow of the Taj. They were unlikely companions, or would have been a few weeks back. But Books was a mine of riveting if useless information. She didn't have a photographic memory quite, but it wasn't far off. They'd teamed up because she'd wanted one last visit to the mausoleum before the truck departed and nobody but Tommy had been available to go with her. The hassle in the narrow lanes outside the Taj could prove too much for some girls on their own, like Books; with a man along, it was bearable, even if he was wearing United's away strip. She'd been reciting the attendances at every World Cup Final since its inauguration in 1930.

'M-Y-C-O-C-K.' The youth craned himself to peer at the logo on Tommy's vest, treating the adventurers to a blast of halitosis that would have stripped paint.

'Christian name or surname?' Books rolled over to blink at the gangling loon from the owlish security of her spectacles. She never wore shades.

'Pardon me?'

'First name or last name?'

'It's the family name,' Mycock affirmed proudly. 'First Mycock came over with the Pilgrim Fathers in 1827. My given name is in remembrance of a famous European composer. My folks kind of hoped I'd become a musician.' He looked abject for a moment. 'Guess I kind of let them down.'

Books sank back and tossed out names, sensibly going for the more grotesque combinations first. 'Beethoven. Beethoven Mycock? Shostakovich. Does he count as European? Shostakovich Mycock?' She shot an eye open to catch the boy tugging on a rubbery zit. Mycock shook his head in smug denial. 'Uh, okay . . . Chopin, Liszt, Tchaikovsky.' Mycock continued working on the zit. 'Hmm, Let's think. Wagner . . . Holst . . . Rav . . .' She paused as if stunned and then flumped her double chins upwards in disbelief. 'GOT IT! My God, I don't believe it! HANDEL MYCOCK. That's who you are!'

'That's my name. Don't wear it out.' Handel leaned forward to extend a leprous arm.

The road from Agra to Kathmandu cut through Madhya Pradesh, Khajuraho and Varanasi. The fecundity and comparative wealth of Rajastan was left quickly behind and for two days the adventurers were exposed to a part of India that packaged tourists choose to fly over. Sprouting vegetation seemed at times to have overwhelmed everything save the sorry track which cut across the landscape. Thatched huts and Hindu temples, squeaking pigs and naked children were glimpsed periodically, in the final throes of being swallowed by the foliage. Once, in a squalid patch that might only be optimistically described as a clearing, thirty to forty vultures flapped and feasted on the carcass of a recently expired water buffalo. Tucked in beneath its belly, a litter of podgy, tan-coloured pups jostled over its flesh, unconscious of their ferocious dining companions. A shuffling pig trotted away from the scene into the undergrowth, a glossy crow perched triumphantly upon its back, its beak wending this way and that, as if to display its cleverness in obtaining a free ride. Occasionally, stones were thrown by the village kids, more to break the tedium of their lives than to demonstrate any political point.

They camped just off the road, in a rough lay-by between villages. Old Nick kept them entertained at night, plucking on a guitar he'd picked up in Agra.

'Promise me two things,' the university boy who had clinched the deal had murmured. 'Never sell it because you will always regret the sale and always wash your hands and remove your shoes before you play. It sounds ridiculous to you, I know,' the lad had continued earnestly, 'but it feels and plays better if you do this. You are playing with a pure heart.'

'Arsehole of the world, man.' That's how Handel had endearingly described Varanasi to Tommy back at the Taj and as the truck laboured through the streets banked with human debris, Tommy saw why. Filthy gutters teemed with rats and garbage, infiltrating the packed cardboard homes along the sidewalk. A ragtag rabble of urchins pursued the truck relentlessly, yelling shrilly to its occupants as they clung for a foothold: 'Gimme rupee, gimme bonbon. Gimme rupee, gimme bonbon. Gimme, gimme!'

An overnighter, that's all Haggis had planned for the city. Up before dawn to catch the faithful at the Ganges and then down the road to Nepal. Promptly at six, a fleet of taxis ferried the adventurers to the tourist ghats in time for sunrise. Two boats were commandeered and in seconds their captains had poled away from the quayside and were floating downriver. To Tommy's right, the human anthill had tipped itself to the very brink of the bank and beyond. Scrawny women, chattering like sparrows, squatted above the waterline and scrubbed their laundry on the worn, green stones. Fat, meaty women sloshed water beneath their cavernous armpits and roared with gusto. Men defecated unashamedly into the black waters as their comrades scooped palmfuls of

131

the holy liquid into their mouths, in lieu of toothpaste. Periodically, sad bodies burned on lonely ghats.

And then the sun, a massive golden globe, began to stretch, as if fresh-wakened from the far horizon. It illuminated the entire landscape as it pushed upwards, first as a crescent of red balloon and finally as a huge, perfect, life-giving ball, bobbling about barely above the skyline. Tommy glanced to his right, intrigued as to whether this phenomenon would pall for those who performed their ablutions daily. He let out a long exhalation of breath. Serried ranks of the devout had broken from their worldly chores and were stretching silently facing their source of light in a strange posture of prayer. Jenny, who knew a thing or two about this, caught Tommy's gasp and whispered reverently into his ear: 'Yoga. It's the Salute to the Sun. I'll show you how at the next truckstop.'

Back at the quayside, a number of cremations were in progress. Poppy thought the pyres abnormally small but was informed by Werner that the amount of wood was strictly determined. Several of the corpses, he thought aloud, must have had a very recent expiry date. They seemed scarcely to have ceased breathing. 'Ah, we Hindus have a desire to remove the soul from this earth and away to happiness very quickly,' a stoker interrupted. 'This cremation process takes only three hours. Much quicker than you westerners,' he smirked.

'It's about the only thing you do do quickly,' grunted Blondie, as the adventurers hauled themselves onto the truck and into Nepal.

9

BANG YOUR BOOTS AND EVEREST

At Sonauli, the border crossing, the company left behind a surging, unstoppable wave of poverty and hopelessness. They found in Nepal a land of polite men in party hats whose children substituted, with outstretched palm, 'Medicines, please,' for 'Gimme rupee, gimme, gimme . . .'

Everything changed. The Nepalese were petite and Mongolian in appearance. Their skin seemed to have been dealt with less harshly by the sun. Dwellings, two storeys high, topped by overlapping thatches, became the order of the day. From balconied verandahs, smiling women greeted the adventurers. Between villages, hectares of mature trees flourished, tomorrow's precious fuel in all its glory.

They loaded up on fruit at Narayanghat, taking aboard also a selection of cooked delicacies from the scatter of wayside stalls. Haggis had suggested that if they had the inclination to get loaded, then Kukri rum might be the best for the job. It was a rich, dark, fiery concoction and almost everyone tucked half a bottle away. But the fact that astonished them all, above the beauty of the surrounding foothills and the ragged whiteness of the Annapurnas beyond, was that not once in Narayanghat were they molested, pulled about or pestered. The change had come without warning, like a sudden crack to the forehead. Rather than a source of plunder, the Nepalese preferred to regard the adventurers as passing cabaret, twentieth century jongleurs-on-wheels.

The crossing point into Chitwan, the Royal National Park, was a shallow but fast-flowing stream, less than thigh deep but powerful enough to send small rocks tumbling along its current. Their two-day stay was an extra, a result of good time-keeping and careful husbandry on Haggis's part. 'I'd expect nothing else from a Jock,' Cap had grinned.

Tottering about at three thirty the next morning, Tommy viewed the side trip with unease. The adventurers had hired a local guide to whisk them through the park before sunrise in the hope of catching the wildlife at play. There were sambar, spotted deer, one-horned rhinos, thirty Bengal tigers and the elephants.

The villages around the perimeter of the park were coming to life around 4 a.m. It was still dark and dewy but the occasional hurricane lamp flared or dog barked. From out of the mist, blanketed figures uttered a scarcely perceptible 'Namaste' in greeting before trudging back to their wood-gathering.

The trail tagged alongside a stream before ending abruptly and continuing on the far side. What was needed, Tommy decided, was a series of stepping stones or logs that would enable the party to negotiate the water silently and without a soaking. With this in mind, he caught up with the guide at the head of their tame little safari.

Around the next bend, Tommy saw precisely what he had been looking for. Three or four large boulders rose presumptuously out of the water at regular intervals. They would transport the adventurers to within three metres of the opposite bank and there, halving the distance between the final stone and the far side, was an old, rotting log. It lay horizontally in the water, perfect for stepping onto. Tommy tugged at the guide's arm, grinning yellowly with his unwashed teeth and darted ahead.

It took a fair few seconds before the guide divined his intention. Tommy had already scrambled down the slope and leapt onto the first of the conveniently placed boulders. The guide's cry rang out as he prepared to launch himself onto the second.

'NOOOOOO!' Vigorously, the little Nepali waved Tommy back to the slope. This done, he picked up a weighty stick from beside the track. The remainder of the group had caught up and encircled him by now, waiting for explanation.

The stick was a hefty piece of wood, about the length and thickness of a man's arm and bent slightly in the middle, where the elbow might be. Sucking in a deep breath, the guide drew back his throwing arm and prepared to hurl the stick. The projectile went whacking through the air, cartwheeling more rapidly as it gained momentum. It thudded dully against the tip of the log, causing a slight splash as one end dipped into the water. To the group's astonishment, the log raised itself, swished its body in a lumbering reptilian fashion and pushed off out of sight into deeper water.

The guide turned to the open-mouthed assembly, a faint smile playing on his lips. 'Marsh mugger,' he explained. 'King Croc in Chetwan.'

The group stumbled on, with Tommy keeping well to the rear. Before the sun had risen finally in the sky, they had observed countless birds, spotted deer and an elephant. Still feeling somewhat drained after his encounter with the marsh mugger, Tommy lugged it back to base, his boots and woolly socks sopping.

Later, down by the river bank, Tommy eased himself

backwards onto the grass and gazed upon a clear sky. Kathmandu lay a day or so away now and he and Poppy still had no clear idea of their intentions. A few metres to his left, a trio of raven-haired Nepali girls bathed, stripped to the waist. They didn't do that alongside the edges of the Manchester Ship Canal. Further along, a couple of working elephants prepared to ford the river, clearly at a point where the waters ran more deeply. Each bore goods strapped to its prodigious back and the larger beast, the one in the lead, balanced its master upon its corrugated neck. Tommy watched as they plopped then waded into midstream. The first beast sank to within inches of the produce on its laden back and then climbed ponderously into shallower waters. Its diminutive companion plodded obediently in its wake until its head and shoulders were completely submerged. Only its cargo rose above the water level, never deviating from the fixed line set by the first beast. Baby emerged with stately dignity seconds later and lumbered on towards the shale of the far bank without breaking a stride. Tommy thought back to the containers churning up the M62, to Flegg and Grobbo and all the screaming kids he'd left behind in the comprehensive, a galaxy or so away. Blinking at the sunlight, he sank back and closed his eyes.

Cap and his family awoke him, shortly before noon. Alison had spotted a mysterious hump basking in a section of still water, sheltered by the opposite bank. She double-checked that it was neither of the Bolsterleys, relaxing after a mid-morning blow-out, and then scurried off to inform her father. Cap surmised that it might be the elusive one-horned rhino.

Pricked by interest, Tommy sat up, ready to take part in the proceedings. The far shore lay thirty, perhaps forty metres away and the beast was a good hundred metres downstream. As things stood, there was little hope of a decent view, let alone a photograph.

Like an officer of the Special Boat Service, Cap set out, taking to the water on his covert mission. With camera held aloft, he swam backstroke, using his free arm, barely rippling the water with each powerful stroke. The current ballooned him outwards, as he intended, and he beached a bare fifty metres away from the dozing hulk beyond.

'For Christ's sake, be careful, Al!' Jenny yelled but her husband was too intent on his stealthy mission to notice. As with Blondie over the incident of the water back in Syria, nicknames were quickly cast aside when the situation merited it. Cap stalked the beast expertly, keeping to the bush for the first thirty metres, then dropping to the water's edge for the final approach. The rhino remained immobile.

At ten metres, Cap paused to cock his camera. A stickler for detail, he adjusted and re-adjusted the focus and insisted on setting the speed and aperture on manual. With camera satisfactorily primed, Cap waded a pace further.

The beast heaved out of the water like some primordial nightmare, bursting into life after a billion years in limbo. Its colossal head panned round in annoyance at the minor irritation before it. Even on the far bank, Jenny felt she could see it glower.

'AL-A-A-N!' she wailed, picking up a pebble to throw at the monster. 'Come back, for Christ's sake!'

'Hey, mum,' Alison interrupted, 'do you remember that guy at Mailbin Zoo? When that hippo trod on him, it crushed him clean in half.'

'Shaddap, Allie!' Jenny barked, reaching for a further handful of ammunition. 'Alan, come back!'

But Cap, in an astonishing mix of courage and foolhardiness, was swishing even further towards the beast. Water lapped about his knees and it became clear to Tommy that if the animal charged, Cap would have no chance. It was at that awkward depth where running was a silly, sploshing affair and swimming was impossible.

'It took the keepers two days to clear up the mess,' Alison persisted. Jenny swung round in pain and parted the air just above her head. Cap, meanwhile, had taken a few considered steps further and was now eyeballing the rhino from what Tommy adjudged to be about five metres. After what seemed an interminable pause, he craned his camera upwards, until the viewfinder was level with his eyes. The rhino bobbed its head fractionally but refrained from charging. Jenny looked ashen.

'This kid at school saw it squash him. Whoomp! All the guts spilled.' Tommy caught Alison's shoulder and squeezed it. She was trembling no less than her mother.

Over on the far side, Cap held the camera tantalisingly in position then drew it down to his body. He stilled himself and the eyeballing continued. Then, almost imperceptibly, he began to withdraw, never allowing his eyes to leave the beast. At twenty metres, Jenny let out a gasp of relief. As the waters rippled over his shorts, Cap fell back into the stream and backstroked lazily towards them. As if it had been cheapened somehow by this brush with tourism, the rhino slushed disgruntedly from its pool and lumbered into the foliage.

Cap stepped out of the water about thirty seconds later, his eyes twinkling like sunlight bouncing off the water.

'You can take that shit-eating grin off your face,' Jenny coughed, her voice still rough with emotion. 'And if you ever do that again . . .' She threw her arms about him and squeezed as Alison stood a pace or so behind, biting her lip and pulling at her cheek with her sleeve.

That evening, back at the restaurant, Tommy related the little ditty he had composed to remind him of his flirtation with leg surgery. He coughed to clear his throat and began. 'Ahem *The Marsh Mugger.*

The Marsh Mugger's
A harsh bugger
King Croc of all Chetwan
His best disguise
A log with eyes
One snap and then you're gone!'

There was a creaky round of applause, the slapping of a beer glass or two against the tablecloth and somebody pushed a shot of Kukri in his direction. He glanced at Poppy for a reprimand but she had chosen diplomatically to fix her eyes on the electric fan swishing silently above their heads.

A party had been planned for the following evening, a big farewell bash, but beyond that there was nothing on the agenda. After three months of intense relationships, the group would peel away, restricting itself to the interchange of Christmas cards and the occasional aerogramme for a year or so. One of the hardest things would be the disappearance of Poppy and the re-emergence of Mum. Tommy wondered whether it would happen in a swift fall in Kathmandu or in a gradual, almost unconscious descent. Blondie's transgressions with the water purifying tabs appearing to have been forgiven and he and Nokkers would probably go on together, Tommy decided, playing those adult games of Doctors and Nurses which so eluded him. It was easy and enjoyable at four, slipping a doctor's white coat over your shoulders and running your hands over a little friend's body, plastic stethoscope trailing from your ears. He'd still been playing it at seven, Tommy ruminated, though a year later he'd swapped his medical training for a season ticket and had never looked back. Those early skills appeared to have deserted him and he was keen to know

139

when they'd return. The families, of course, would stick together. Cap would be leading his tribe back to Koonoomoo whilst the Bolsterleys had completed only the first stage of their global foray. Switzerland would be denied their company for a further two and a half years. Sally and Haggis would set to work for a fortnight, refitting the truck before escorting a fresh party of adventurers from Nepal on the return leg to London. A couple of the single girls were flying home; they'd sliced three months out of their lives, away from hospital wards and office desks and their time was up. But they'd be changed forever. Poppy and Tommy remained, as yet, without definite plans.

Over the previous three months, Tommy had jawed periodically with west-bound travellers about Kathmandu and thus it was not surprising that on arrival he felt he already knew it well. As the truck wheezed to a halt on Kantipath, he sprang out, knowing the GPO was on the corner.

Most of the adventurers jumped out too, eager to collect their accumulated mail from the circus inside the Post Office's green doors. The majority had booked in already to the Blue Star, a tourist hotel on the Patan side of town. The less affluent, Tommy and Poppy included, headed for the travellers' area, Thamel, where basic facilities were available at a sixth of the price. The Nicks, Big and Old, operating on a rock bottom budget, had steered in the direction of the flop-houses operating along Freak Street. All avowed to meet up at Utse's, the Tibetan restaurant, the following night for their final bash together.

Tommy and Poppy shared a room at the Dreamland, a 30-rupee joint above the Zen restaurant. The room itself was Spartan but clean. Tommy threw the shutters open and the sound of a flute drifted in from the balcony opposite. Below, bullocks and dogs danced about men with party hats whilst women prepared themselves for the opening of street markets. Tommy inhaled deeply. The air smelt magical.

They breakfasted next morning at the Delicacy, a leisurely feast of muesli with curd and fruit and chewy pancakes laced with cheese and local honey. On the next table, bushy mountaineers earnestly discussed their last ascent in terminology which eluded the Granites. There was no hurry, no truck to catch, just a lazy day spreading before them in which to savour Kathmandu.

Poppy had correspondence to write back at the Dreamland so Tommy left her after a second coffee and strolled down the bustling thoroughfare of Indrachowk. It was a place to rub shoulders with travellers and locals in equal proportions. Secondhand clothing shops flourished, peddling the discarded boots and duvets of hikers returned from the hills. Worn old women, bent under the weight of twenty bundled kilos of wood, lurched from side to side of one of the town's oldest arteries. Cyclists of all nationalities tinkled bells as they cobbled past whilst from windows a technicolor spread of tourist paraphernalia screamed at browsers. Every third or fourth plot was a restaurant and Tommy counted twenty national cuisines being served before he cut off down the river to Swayambunath.

Abruptly, the trappings of tourism ceased and Tommy found himself in the company of Nepalis who lived lives uncomplicated by the dollar bill. He passed ancient squares, buildings of faded brick with latticed shutters, buildings where generations of women had sat sifting pans over piles of grain, the chaff blowing in their hair. Down by the river, isolated, unmourned corpses smouldered on raised spits of shale, around which the water tongued and ran on. From his vantage point on the

141

rickety bridge, Tommy gazed down at them and on the ragged knots of children running through the wide meadows on the stream's far bank.

The monkey temple remains the symbol of Kathmandu. Its golden stupa, at the highest point of the valley, gazes omnisciently upon the faithful. It is square in shape at first and it is on each of the four sides that the legendary eyes have been painted. The stupa then becomes rounded in shape, tapering off to the heavens.

The approach proved quite an effort, even for Tommy, his body corrugated by three months in a confined space. The rising staircase to the temple may not have had too many steps, maybe 200 or so, but each was steep and many were blocked by beggars. Tommy had needed two appreciable breathers before making it to the entrance proper.

At the summit, a Nepali businessman drew him mysteriously to one side, a portly individual sporting a waistcoat, a walrus moustache and a party hat. 'I must apologise, sir, for the level of refuse one is encountering on the approaches today.'

Tommy cocked an eye at him uncertainly and thought back bizarrely to the raked terracing of the Stretford End. 'Oh, I don't know. I didn't see any litter. Try coming to Manchester sometime.'

The businessman's explanation was accompanied by an insistent, synchronised nodding. 'No, no, no, sir. I am not referring to the disposal of waste papers but to the beggarly types disporting themselves idly across the flagstones. They are Indian beggars, sir, and they will not take no for an answer.' His moustache was twitching with emotion.

'Every month it is the same sir. The Indian government rounds up its most disreputable citizens and drives them by the coachload to our border at Sonauli. They pick and

142

cheat their way to Kathmandu and give no peace to businessmen such as myself. Their behaviour is reprehensible and abominable.'

He gazed mournfully at the all-seeing eye, as if for guidance. 'Do not misunderstand me, sir. It is the duty of a good Hindu to give to the poor. But they come in my shop, I give them five rupees and they say it is not enough. They refuse to leave. They are persistent.'

Tommy nodded his head sagely.

'So there is little difficulty in distinguishing between Nepali beggars and the Indian variety, sir. The Nepalis have a better class of beggar altogether.' He dipped his head slightly in valediction and departed, the pupils of his brown eyes still gorged with indignation. Tommy gazed up to the symbol of the valley above him. It was difficult to tell for sure, what with the glare of sun on gold, but he felt he just might have caught its eye winking.

Back at Dreamland, Tommy and Poppy prepared for Utse's.

'Can I use the bathroom first, Mum?' Tommy called. Poppy had had to steel herself to a range of bizarre questioning over the previous three months but this last innocent request made her sway. 'And how about a clean bar of soap? The ones in here are disgusting.'

After three months on the road, there wasn't a lot they'd forgotten about their wardrobes. Decking oneself out in something fresh was out of the question; what was possible was to sport a piece that might have slipped temporarily from people's minds. Tommy dug out a denim shirt that he dimly remembered being laundered in Lahore. Poppy spirited a dull green flying suit from her wardrobe, something Tommy hadn't seen since the Channel crossing. Thus, shampooed and pressed, they strolled into Thamel, calling into Rumdoodle's for a pre-nosh drink, as arranged.

Most of the gang were already there, flobbing about on cushions in the upper room. It struck Tommy that he'd never seen them so spruce. There wasn't a T-shirt or uncombed lock in the place; even Haggis had seen fit to curb the ginger excesses above his upper lip. They wouldn't have looked too outlandish in an English wine bar on a wet Saturday afternoon.

The bar didn't take too much trade off the adventurers, though, for most had starved themselves during the day in anticipation of the blow-out at Utse's and in less than half an hour they were seated at the best eating-house in town.

Poppy took her place next to Tommy who was wedged somewhat in a corner and they shared a glance at the menu. Its listings were exclusively Tibetan and completely without explanation. It was a time to throw culinary caution to the winds. The waitresses edged about, squeezing behind high-backed chairs, and pencilled down the laborious orders of the rash band before them.

Twenty beers thumped upon the tables, a parting shot from Haggis, and the celebrations began. Poppy would never have allowed her son a full glass back in England but, over the months, a gradual shift had taken place. She blew the froth off Tommy's glass and smiled. Nokkers, who had surreptitiously been collecting a variety of currency from the group over the past few days, produced a heavily-strapped parcel from Blondie's relieved lap and thrust it into the striped paunch of her podgy courier. 'That's from all of us, mate. You're not half bad, for a Pom!' She leaned over and lathered his cheeks with a sloppy brace of kisses. A ragged cheer erupted. Marc-Marc presented Sally with an inscribed tyre-jack: THANKS FOR THE LIFT and then the food arrived.

144

'Momos?' the beaming waitress enquired, lowering a plate of what appeared to be anaesthetised slugs to the table. 'Momos?' She drew a blank as the adventurers struggled to hold down their breakfasts. On the platter, half a dozen momos slithered unhappily, as if guiltily aware of their reprieve.

At about eleven, when there was a very real danger of the adventurers chuting under the table, Haggis suggested the casino. It lay on the outskirts of town and admission, like the return taxi fare, was free. The notion hit them like a second wind and within minutes they were bundled into the taxis pulling up sharp outside Utse's.

There was not much to choose between the casino and a downmarket night spot in Blackpool. Its carpets and fabrics must once have been plush but those days were long gone. There were no high-rolling international spies cruising here or dripping femmes fatales to hang on one's shoulders. Peculiarly, as he entered the foyer, leaving the 'Dollars Only' room for the Germans, Tommy had a vision of a spindly, rheumy-eyed mystic on a Delhi sidewalk. Words swam through his head: POPPY . . . CHRYSANTHEMUM . . . RUBBER PLANT. And then there was the sensation of three numbers pulsing behind his eyelids: 4, 26 and 12. Tommy felt dizzy for an instant but the moment passed and his head cleared.

He mooched around with Poppy at first, sussing out the odds before exchanging his ten-dollar stake for a palmful of plastic. In Europe, of course, he wouldn't have made it beyond the doorway but in Nepal, in this different life, it didn't seem to matter. He was white and he had money to lose. There was blackjack, pontoon, beat the dealer and roulette, plus a table or two of less familiar games. Excited knots of tourists hung about: Indians, mostly, staying at the airport hotel. It was the women, Tommy noticed, who placed the majority of bets, drawing an endless supply of cheap blue chips from beneath the folds of coloured shawls. Their menfolk appeared to patronise them, standing aside with an air of faint disdain.

'Mum, I keep getting this strange feeling.' Tommy ground the words out, squeezing Poppy's hand as he did so.

She nuzzled his ear with her hot, becreepered nose.

'The loos are over there, by the coffee stand.'

'Four, twenty six and twelve.' He did a passable impersonation of Leroy's mum, Rosetta. 'It's the old psychic powers at work.'

'Psychotic, more like,' she grinned good-humouredly and sauntered in the direction of the blackjack.

Adopting what he considered to be a nonchalant pose, Tommy strolled theatrically to the roulette table and angled himself above the heads of the punters to assess the state of play. There were about a dozen gamblers, all small fry save for a distinguished gent of middle age. He was Indian in origin, a silver-haired Hindu, and he gave the impression of having strayed by accident from the 'Dollars Only' room. As most of the players agonised over the placement of their ten-cent chips, the high roller was clumping unsteady piles of golden octagons on the board, apparently at random. He must have staked the equivalent of $150, Tommy estimated. The bearing skitted coltishly about the wheel, coming to settle on '4'. Silverstrands betrayed no emotion at his loss. Impassively, he delved into his tailored pocket and produced a second palmful of plastic gold.

Poppy came up beside Tommy, nuzzling her chin along his shoulder. 'Guess what just won.' The words uncoiled in serpentine manner from the near side of his pressed lips.

'Thirty seven?' quizzed Poppy hopefully. 'Just a wild

guess.'

'It'd have a job,' Tommy hissed. He glared accusingly at his mum and breathed conspiratorially into her ear. 'Four.'

Already the ball was skittering around again. Beside the wheel, the table was sloppily bestrewn with stakes, the old man's pile of gold dwarfing the puny efforts of his rivals. They were as luxury apartments, skyscrapers in Toytown, surrounded by ghettoes of lowly bungalows. The ball decelerated, bobbed, braked hard, then bobbed once more. Twenty six.

Tommy pinned his fingers about his mum's ample waist and squeezed hard. Really hard. There would still be accusing red marks there in the morning.

'Mum. I know you'll think I'm crazy but I want all my spends on Number 12. Now.'

The pupils in his eyes looked set to explode as his bony fingers enmeshed themselves even more urgently into Poppy's fleshy padding.

'My money. All of it. The whole year's. I don't care. Do it now.'

As in a dream, Poppy turned in the direction of the cashier's desk. From her belt, she extracted $250, Tommy's spends for a year. A mountain of octagonal plastic was pushed her way. She scooped them with a spread palm and floated back to Tommy. The entire transaction had been completed wordlessly.

'Here you are, Tom. You've been saying how you've been fancying chips for a while.' They cascaded noisily into his open hands. 'These should keep you going.' Her eyes never left him as he deposited them in neat piles on the gambling square reserved for Number 12. His eyebrows and lashes, Poppy noticed, were now completely blond. This was not the skitty kid who had jived around the pavements of the Sussex Plaza.

147

Cap, who was passing, tapped him on the shoulder, and extended a hand. 'It's been great knowing you Granites,' he grinned. 'You've got the address. Maybe see you in Koonoomoo sometime. If not, have a good life.' Tommy returned the grip and made his farewells. Poppy gave Cap one of her special hugs.

The ball, which had been positively whistling around the wheel, was making a louder, more infrequent clatter. It was approaching the end of its course.

'Hey, Tommy!' A hand raked him vigorously across the scalp. Blondie and Nokkers stood there, grinning hugely. 'Joined an expedition, Tommy,' Nokkers chirped. 'Leaving for Everest base camp the day after tomorrow. There's a couple of spare places.' She jerked her hand in the direction of his mum.

'Thanks, I'll bear . . .'

'AAAAAAGH! You've won! You've won!' Poppy's eyes were ricocheting about her sockets like demented pinballs. The silver bearing had plopped irrevocably on 12 and a plastic ski-slope of chips was slithering his way.

'Had a bit of luck, Tommy?' Haggis sniffed, shaking his snake-like locks from across the table. 'Not bad, not bad. Come on, it's time you bought me a beer.'

'Two hundred and fifty dollars,' Nick mused, 'at 35 to 1.' By unspoken agreement, after that eyewatering encounter in Lahore, the adventurers had ceased to prefix Nick's name with an adjective. It was plain Nick and Old Nick now. 'I make that eight thousand, seven hundred and fifty dollars.' Nick paused to plonk himself down on the soft, velvety cushion of a barstool. It brought him down to Tommy's sphere of operations, eyeball to eyeball, as a trickle of adventurers gathered round to gape.

'Wheee!' screamed Poppy, scraping a handful of chips off the table and casting them extravagantly upwards.

'Wheeee! Wheeee!'

'Tommy, Tommy, got a number for me?' Books' fingers flexed like clamps about his shaking arm.

'Gizza clue, Tom!'

'Tommy, Tommy!'

'Same again?' Nokkers had him arrested by the shoulder.

'Tommy!'

'Tommy!'

But Tommy's mind was far away now. He wasn't thinking of designer clothes or a CD player or an executive box at Old Trafford. He was thinking of Everest.